Fort Hatred

A puff of gun smoke erupted from the broken window and Moran fired at it without seeming to aim. A bullet whined past his head and he fired two more shots through the window while moving for cover at the right hand side of the shack. A man emerged at a run from the ramshackle building, triggering a stream of lead at Moran, who dropped to one knee, his gun replying with deadly accuracy.

The man fell face down in the dust and did not move again. Moran got up and ran to the front window. He saw movement there and tossed a slug into it. A man pitched to the floor inside the shack. Moran reached the window, gasping, breath searing his throat, shoulders heaving. Sweat was running down his face.

'Hold your fire, Soldier-boy,' Shorten yelled from inside. 'My two men are down and done for. They started shooting against my orders. I ain't fool enough to tangle with the Army while I'm working for them.'

'Come out of the shack with your hands up,' Moran rasped. . . .

Fort Hatred

Corba Sunman

 A Black Horse Western

ROBERT HALE

© Corba Sunman 2017
First published in Great Britain 2017

ISBN 978-0-7198-2512-5

The Crowood Press
The Stable Block
Crowood Lane
Ramsbury
Marlborough
Wiltshire SN8 2HR

www.bhwesterns.com

Robert Hale is an imprint
of The Crowood Press

Typeset by
Derek Doyle & Associates, Shaw Heath
Printed and bound in Great Britain by
CPI Group (UK) Ltd, Croydon, CR0 4YY

ONE

Captain Slade Moran reined in on the crest of a ridge in West Texas and gazed intently at his surroundings. The terrain was featureless, seemingly empty, and a line of mountains, purpled by distance, overpowered the flat landscape with their height and might, but he knew the area from a previous visit and reckoned that he was within spitting distance of Fort Tipton, where he was heading, but first he wanted to check out the nearby town of Cactusville. He was attached to the Provost Corps of the Army of the Interior, and his job was to capture, arrest and bring to trial soldiers who had broken military law.

He saw a cloud of dust off to his right. That must be the trail to the fort, he thought, and if it led into Cactusville then Fort Tipton would be three miles to the north. He urged his tired black horse forward and rode in the direction of the fast-moving wagon he had spotted. He was hunting a renegade cavalryman – Trooper Clark, who had deserted the fort three weeks before, having killed a sentry in the process.

Ordinarily, a deserter would make fast tracks to put as much distance as possible between himself and the unit in which he had served, but it was rumoured that Clark had a woman in Cactusville and was seen in the area since his desertion. When he deserted, Clark had broken out of the guardhouse and killed a sentry who surprised him in the act of taking a horse to further his escape.

Moran was tall, three inches over six feet; lean and well-muscled. He was aged thirty years, blond-haired, and had blue eyes. His civilian store suit was black, trail-worn and dusty, and he wore ankle length leather shoes. His military campaign hat was pulled low over his eyes, and a yellow neckerchief was knotted at his throat. He was armed with a .45 Army Colt, snug on his right hip in a cutaway holster, and a six-shot Springfield carbine in his saddle scabbard.

He rode down a slope and headed for the dust of the wagon he had seen, alert and ready, watching for trouble, and when he caught a furtive movement off to his left, he slipped his feet out of his stirrups. A shot crashed, and Moran dived out of the saddle, reaching for his pistol as he hit the sun-baked ground. The shot echoed as he prepared to fight. His hat was jerked from his head as if by an invisible hand and another series of echoes fled to the horizon. He pushed himself to one knee and cocked his gun.

A figure was running towards him from the brush, sunlight glinting on a hand gun it was holding. The gun lifted to cover Moran and Moran triggered his Colt. The man jerked and twisted away. His legs lost their strength and he blundered to the ground and stretched out in the dust.

Moran got to his feet, his ears ringing. He looked around, but saw no more danger. He reloaded his pistol before picking up his hat, and gazed at the neat bullet hole in the curved brim before moving to the downed man. He kicked an outstretched foot without reaction. Blood was showing on the man's chest. Closer examination showed that he was dead.

Moran straightened and, as he glanced around, he heard the sound of approaching hoof beats – about six horses, and the next instant, half a dozen riders swept into view from the brush and came galloping towards him, guns in their hands. The foremost of the men was wearing a law badge that glinted in the sunlight. They closed in around him and sat their mounts in a rising cloud of dust, covering him with their weapons. One of the men slipped out of leather, came to Moran, and snatched the gun from his hand.

'What's going on here?' demanded the man with the badge. He was tall and solid, with a pistol holstered on his right hip. His dark eyes were filled with suspicion as he regarded Moran. His voice was rough, laced with an innate thread of brutality.

'I was riding into town and this jasper sprang out of the brush shooting at me,' Moran replied. 'I was about to check him out when you showed up.'

'That's short and sweet! Tell me your name and

state your business.'

'I'm Captain Moran – Military Provost Department. I'm on my way to Fort Tipton to take up a case of murder and to hunt down a deserter.'

'Have you got papers on you?'

Moran produced his papers and handed them over. The marshal looked through them intently, and his manner changed appreciably as he returned them.

'I'm glad to make your acquaintance, Captain. I'm Marshal Bowtell of Cactusville. My posse is on the trail because four men raided the bank in town a short time ago and headed out in this direction. One of the robbers had his horse shot from under him, and I reckon it was the guy you shot. Have you seen anyone, apart from this man?'

'Not a soul until that jasper popped out of the brush. Have you any idea who he is?'

'Do you know who he is, Billy?' demanded Bowtell of the man who had taken Moran's gun.

'Never see him before,' Billy replied.

'Give the Captain his gun back and we'll be on our way.' Bowtell touched the brim of his Stetson. 'I'll see you around if you're gonna spend some time in town. Leave that bozo lying where he is and we'll pick him up when we return. I'll check him out. So long!'

The posse moved out, leaving Moran standing beside the dead man. When the sound of hoof beats faded, Moran dropped to one knee beside the body and searched its pockets. He found nothing, and fetched his horse and loaded the dead man behind the cantle. He mounted and rode on until he came upon a trail that led north and south, chose north and pushed his mount into a lope. Minutes later, he caught a glimpse of buildings ahead, and pulled his black off to the left in order to circle the town. He realized that he needed to visit Fort Tipton as a priority to get the lowdown on the deserter Robert Clark, and an identity for the dead man who had attacked him.

He saw the fort a mile before he reached it, and a sigh of relief escaped him when he reached the big double gate and halted where a sentry was standing in the shade with a carbine in his hands.

'Have you got business in the fort?' the sentry demanded.

'I'm Captain Moran, Military Provost. I'm here to see Colonel Davis.'

The sentry came to attention and saluted. 'Yes, sir, Captain. Go through the gates, sir, and cross the parade square to the headquarters building. There'll be a sentry on the veranda. He'll take you to First Sergeant Craven in the Troop Office, who will take you to Major Harmon, in command because the Colonel is off sick.'

'You're a mine of information, Sentry. What's your name?'

'Belding, sir. Welcome to Fort Hatred, Captain.'

'This is Fort Tipton, isn't it?'

Belding grinned. 'The men have a better name for it, Captain.'

'Take a look at the dead man behind my saddle,

Belding, and tell me if you know him.'

Belding came forward and lifted the dead man's head by grasping the hair and twisting it. He gazed at the dead features, then let go of the hair and looked up into Moran's grim face.

'He's a stranger to me, Captain. How did you get him, sir?'

Moran smiled and rode into the fort without answering. The parade ground stretched before him and he crossed it to a row of wooden buildings on the far side. A sentry stood in the shade of a veranda, and came forward as Moran dismounted and dragged the body off the horse.

'I'm Captain Moran. I want to see whoever is in command.'

'Yes, sir.' The sentry saluted. 'That'll be Major Harmon, Captain. You'll find the First Sergeant in the Troop office, through the second door, sir. He'll put you right.'

'Get an orderly to take care of my horse,' Moran said. 'I shall be staying here for some days. Have my blanket roll taken to the officers' quarters.'

'First Sergeant Craven will attend to your needs, Captain.'

Moran mounted the veranda and entered the doorway the sentry had indicated. He found himself in the Troop Office, which contained two desks, shelves lined with folders and stationary. Two men were seated at the desks. One wore the stripes of a First Sergeant; a short, older man with greying hair cut very short. His uniform was immaculate. His face was weathered by the sun and he looked as if he could handle anything that came up in the line of duty. His brown eyes were alert, and when he looked up from his paperwork and saw Moran, he got immediately to his feet and stiffened to attention, a smile crossing his lips and instantly disappearing from his face.

'Captain Moran, sir,' he greeted in a clipped tone. 'It's good to see you again, sir.'

Moran studied the Sergeant-Major's face, and smiled when recognition came to him. 'First Sergeant Craven! I last saw you in Nevada – a pay master and his coach carrying a pay roll had disappeared. I've got a body outside. He ambushed me – I think he was after my horse.'

'You killed him, Captain?' There was no emotion in Craven's voice and his face remained expressionless.

'I had no choice. I'm here to look for Trooper Clark. Bring me up to date on his case, and I'd like to see a summary of evidence. My information about him is that he's hiding out in this area, probably in the town. Have there been any more sightings of him?'

'There are reports that he hasn't left the area, sir. Major Harmon will be able to give you more on that. I'll tell the Major you're here. He'll want to see you as soon as possible.'

'I'll be staying at the fort. My gear is on my horse. Take care of it for me.'

'Will do, sir. I'll appoint an orderly to you. I'll see

if Major Harmon can see you now, Captain.'

Craven went to a door at the rear of the room which bore the legend Commanding Officer, knocked, and entered in response to a harsh voice calling an order to enter. Moran turned and looked out through a window beside the outer door. A dozen mounted troopers were now lined up on the square and a sergeant, also mounted, was shouting drill orders. The Sergeant-Major emerged from the office.

'Major Harmon will see you now, Captain.'

Moran entered the inner office and a tall figure stood up behind a desk set before a large window and came forward, his right hand outstretched.

'Captain Moran,' he said. 'I'm pleased to meet you. I've heard a lot about you, and we could certainly do with your help around here.'

Major Harmon was tall and lean, his long face showing the unmistakable signs of worry, especially around the eyes. His uniform was smartly pressed and his boots were highly polished. His thick black moustache softened the line of his taut mouth which showed a tendency to cruelty. His eyes had no compassion – they were like black pebbles from the bottom of a stagnant creek.

'Welcome to Fort Tipton, Captain. First Sergeant Craven will bring you up to date on Clark. Please excuse me but I have an appointment to see some of the town committee in Cactusville, and I'm running late. I'll catch up with you when I get back from town and we'll plan a clean sweep in this area to regain the initiative lost by Colonel Davis.'

Moran saluted and departed, and was talking to First Sergeant Craven in the outer office when Major Harmon emerged from his office and departed. Craven's craggy face showed a number of expressions, dislike among them, as he gazed after the Major, and Moran noticed but made no comment.

'I'll need Clark's summary of evidence, Sergeant-Major. Then I'll settle into my quarters and get into uniform.'

'I've given Trooper Myhill orders to act as your orderly, Captain. He'll be in your quarters now. He's taken your horse and your gear and should be working on your uniform by this time – if he isn't, he'll be on punishment drill before the day is out.'

'Harsh treatment, Sergeant-Major,' Moran commented.

'Yes, sir.' Craven's face was impassive, but his eyes gleamed. 'Discipline has slackened around here but now the Colonel is out of the way, we can stamp out the trouble that's come up. I've got the matter in hand, Captain.'

Craven opened a drawer in his desk, took out a folder, and held it out to Moran. 'This is the summary of evidence for Trooper Clark. We'll get on with his court martial once you've brought him back – and we'll throw the book at him. With any luck we'll be able to prove that he was the instigator of the murder of Lieutenant Sandwell, who was shot dead on the parade ground a month ago. The fatal shot was fired from outside the fort, Captain, from a spot on Spyglass Hill. By the time we realized that fact, the killer had slipped away, although there were some horse tracks on the Hill.'

'I'll come back to you when I've had a chance to read the summary. I shall need to question all the witnesses who made statements. Now direct me to my quarters and I'll settle in and get down to work.'

Craven called an orderly to show Moran to the officers' quarters.

'And come straight back here, Redfern, when you've shown the Captain where to go,' Craven instructed.

Trooper Redfern turned and left the office, and by the time Moran reached the veranda, Redfern was almost out of sight. Moran called to him and the trooper halted. When Moran reached him, Redfern was standing to attention, his eyes fixed on some invisible spot on the distant horizon.

'Slow it down,' Moran advised. 'What's your hurry?'

'I'm sorry, sir.' Redfern was a short man with an unsmiling face. He was powerfully built around the shoulders, his arms heavily muscled; hands abnormally large. He had blue eyes that glittered with an unholy light, and looked at Moran with none of the submissiveness of a lower rank faced by an officer, but there was no defiance in his direct gaze. He fell into step with Moran. 'I heard tell you're here to hunt down Trooper Clark, Captain.'

'What's your interest in Clark?'

'He was a friend of mine, sir.'

'Why did he desert? I heard he was a good soldier who suddenly kicked over the traces and made a run for it, and yet it's said that he hasn't left the area. What's keeping him here where it's highly dangerous? Deserters usually put as much distance as they can from their point of desertion. Is it true that he's got a woman in Cactusville?'

'He never mentioned anything like that to me, Captain. He didn't just desert. If he hadn't upped-stakes and made a run for it he would have been killed.'

'Like Lieutenant Sandwell?'

'I don't know anything about that, sir. The lieutenant's death had nothing to do with the trouble inside the fort. He was shot from outside by someone on Spyglass Hill.'

'I shall want to talk to you later, after I've picked up what information I can glean from the summary of evidence.'

'That will get you nowhere, sir. The men who know the truth haven't made any statements, and there's nothing I can tell you, sir. I don't know any more than the rest of the troopers here. Judging by the general talk buzzing the fort, everyone is shocked by what has happened and nobody seems to have any idea what and who is behind it.'

'Someone knows something,' Moran said quietly, 'and I'll track him down before I've done with this place.'

'I've heard of your reputation, Captain, and I guess it'll take someone like you to get the lowdown.'

Redfern showed Moran to his quarters, where an orderly stood inside, removing Moran's uniform from the rolled blanket that had been tied behind the cantle of his horse. Redfern departed swiftly. Moran faced his orderly, who stood to attention beside the bed in the room; a short, slight figure with sharp brown eyes and wispy blond hair.

'I'm Trooper Myhill, Captain,' he reported. 'I'm to be your orderly while you're here. I was just about to spruce up your uniform, sir, and polish your boots.'

'Thank you, Myhill. I've got some reading to do.' Moran threw the summary of evidence on the bed. 'I'd appreciate it if you could rustle up some coffee and food before you do anything else. I've been on the trail for several days and meals were sparse.'

'Certainly, sir. I'll run across to the cook house and get you something.'

Myhill departed in a hurry. Moran looked around at his quarters, which were sparsely furnished. There was a tall cupboard, a small table, and a wash basin in one corner. An upright chair and an easy chair completed the furnishing. Moran removed his jacket and draped it over the back of the chair, sat down, opened the summary of evidence folder, and began to read the contents. He became so engrossed in the evidence that he barely noted Myhill's return until the trooper handed him a spoon and a plate of stew. He had set a tray on the table, and a pot of hot coffee sent out an aroma that soon attracted Moran's attention.

He paused to slake his thirst and eat the stew, and

then continued reading the evidence until he had picked up the gist of the events that surrounded the desertion of Clark and the murder of the sentry who had caught Clark in the act of stealing a mount from the horse lines.

There seemed to be no mystery about the murder. The sentry, Trooper Barlow, on duty at the horse lines, was stabbed when confronting Clark, and had survived long enough to raise the alarm and report that he recognized Clark as the man who had stabbed him. There was a statement from the guard at the main gate that he saw a man scaling the wall of the fort from the inside and fired two shots, but the man dropped over the wall and made good his escape. A subsequent search of the outside area of the fort failed to reveal any sign of the man, alive or dead. It was assumed that he had been Clark, who had got out of the guard house an hour before the murder was committed.

Moran read the evidence several times until he had mentally absorbed it, and came to the conclusion that he would have to catch Clark before he could make any headway in the case. He decided to visit Cactusville as soon as possible, accompanied by a trooper who knew Clark, and try to get a lead on the deserter. He would stay out of uniform so that he would not be conspicuous in the town.

Myhill attended to Moran's uniform and boots and put them in the wardrobe before departing to handle other duties. Moran relaxed as he considered the situation. He was washing at the basin in front of the window when one of the panes of glass shattered and tinkled to the floor. He was so surprised he forgot to duck, and a second window was broken before he heard the sound of the first shot, which was so quiet as to be almost inaudible. But he was not slow in dropping to the floor, and in his haste, his head struck the side of the bed. A curtain seemed to drop over his eyes, and sight and sound faded as he lapsed into unconsciousness. . . .

TWO

A hand shaking his shoulder aroused Moran and he opened his eyes to see Sergeant-Major Craven bending over him. Craven helped him to his feet and eased him onto the bed.

'I was coming to see you, Captain,' Craven said, 'and heard the shots. They came from Spyglass Hill.'

'I was washing in front of the window,' Moran said, pressing a hand against the side of his head where it had made violent contact with the bed. He could feel the stickiness of blood, and his head was aching. 'Send a couple of men out to check the hill. I'll go there myself when I'm able.'

'I'll do better than that,' Craven said. 'I'll send a couple of gallopers towards town with orders to turn and ride back to the hill on the back trail from town. They might just catch the sniper riding back to Cactusville.'

'That's a good idea,' Moran agreed.

Craven hurried from the room. Moran got to his feet. His head was clearing. He bathed the wound, pulled on his jacket and hat, and went out to cross the parade square to the headquarters buildings. Four riders swung into view from the horse lines and went galloping to the main gate in a cloud of dust. Sergeant-Major Craven emerged from his office.

'You look shaken, Captain,' Craven observed. 'Perhaps you should see the post doctor before doing anything else. Lieutenant Cross is in his office. I've got to see him, so I'll walk with you over to his place, if I may.'

'I don't need a doctor, Sergeant-Major. Get my horse brought here and I'll go and take a look around. I'll need a man to accompany me into town – someone who knows Clark well, and if he can be dressed in civilian clothes then so much the better.'

'I know just the man, Captain. He'll be here by the time your horse has been saddled.'

Moran was impatient until he was ready to leave the fort. His horse was brought around from the horse lines by a mounted civilian.

'I'm Sergeant Bessemer, Captain,' the man said, 'and I'll be riding with you. I know Clark like I know my own father. If he's in Cactusville then we'll get him.'

'That's very good, Sergeant.'

Moran liked the appearance of Bessemer, who was large and looked capable of handling anything that might come up. He was fleshy, his face somewhat battered. His nose was crooked, and he had several lumps around his eyebrows. His blue eyes were hard and bright.

'Let's take a look around Spyglass Hill. Someone is getting into the habit of shooting into the fort from there, and he should be discouraged from further activity.'

'Yes, sir. It will be a pleasure. Lieutenant Sandwell was killed on parade by a shot fired from the hill. He was a fine officer, sir – my Troop leader, and I'd like to get the man who killed him.'

They left the fort and rode towards the hill. Moran had a stream of questions to ask and so many points to cover, and he was aware that he could only cover one facet at a time.

'What kind of a man was Sandwell?' he asked.

'The man or the soldier, sir?'

'The man. Did he get drunk in town? Did he gamble? Did he chase after women? Did his involvement with a married woman bring the husband down on him?'

'I don't think he did any of those things, sir. He was just a normal man, and he treated his troop OK, which says a lot about him.'

'But he had one enemy – someone who hated him enough to want to kill him.'

'It could have been someone with a grudge against soldiers generally, and picked him because he was in view at the time when the shot was fired.'

Moran nodded. He looked at Spyglass Hill, which was visible from ground level, and then glanced back at the fort, judging the distance between the summit of the hill and the parade ground inside the fort to be about 500 yards – a long shot, and probably impossible for an ordinary Army long gun. So there had to be a man in the locality who owned a special rifle, probably equipped with a telescopic sight. He had seen several such weapons in his time, and made a note of the fact for further reference.

The hill was no higher than fifty feet, and looked as if the builders of the fort had planned to build earthworks but had not completed the job. As Moran drew closer to the spot, he saw two soldiers scrambling around on the apex; their mounts were grazing nearby. They came down to ground level and joined Moran and Bessemer. One of the two was a sergeant, and he saluted Moran.

'I'm Sergeant Askew, Captain. I sent two of the patrol to ride a wide circle around the hill to look for recent tracks. There's nothing on the hill; not even an empty cartridge case. Was anyone in the fort hit by the shooting, sir?'

'It was directed at me,' Moran replied. 'Some windows were broken, that's all. Wait for the rest of your patrol to return to you. If they have found tracks then send someone to find me in town to report their findings. If there is nothing to report then return to the fort. Sergeant Bessemer and I are riding to town immediately.'

Sergeant Askew saluted. Moran regained his saddle and departed with Bessemer at his side. Bessemer selected their route in such a way that if a rider had left the hill for Cactusville after the shooting then they would be certain to find his tracks. But they found nothing, and as they continued to town, the two gallopers appeared whom Sergeant-Major Craven had sent out, and they reported that they had not found any tracks. The gallopers were ordered to return to the fort, and Moran continued to town.

Cactusville seemed to rise up out of the range as they neared the little community of some 600 souls. There was a collection of buildings on either side of the trail heading south, most of them built of adobe. The general appearance of the place was sad and lonely. There were few people in view, the sun blazed down, and dust was everywhere. An old dog lying in the shade of a broken-down wagon lifted his head to look at them as they passed by, but did not have the energy to get up and check them out. His head dropped back on to his paws and he closed his eyes.

There was some activity in front of the Mercantile. Two men were loading supplies on a buckboard. Three horses were standing hipshot at a hitch rail outside a saloon, and Bessemer reined in.

'Have we got time to wet our whistles, sir?' he asked.

Moran smiled. 'I guess we can check out the saloon first,' he replied, 'and we could quench our thirst while we are inside – all in the name of duty.'

They dismounted and tied their mounts to a hitch rail. Moran led the way into the saloon. Several men were standing at the long bar with glasses before them, and they all turned and looked towards the entrance when they heard the batwings creak. The hum of voices halted as if cut off by a knife. Moran went to the bar and leaned an elbow on it. The bartender, a small, wiry-looking man in a red shirt, had sparse black hair flattened with a liberal dose of pungent-smelling hair oil, the aroma of which preceded him as he came along the bar. He looked from Moran to Bessemer and his face lapsed into a smile.

'What are you doing in town at this time of the day, Sergeant?' he demanded. 'And out of uniform too. Have you deserted?'

'I'm showing a new officer around, Clancy,' Bessemer replied.

'Two beers,' Moran said, and waited until the 'tender slid foaming glasses along the bar. 'What do you know about deserters, Clancy?'

'Nothing but town talk,' Clancy replied, his dark eyes blinking rapidly.

Moran picked up his glass and took a long drink, his keen gaze not leaving the 'tender's face. 'And what are they saying around town?' he persisted.

Clancy shrugged. 'It's mostly nonsense, as usual. Have you come to replace Colonel Davis?'

'No.' Moran lapsed into silence.

Clancy shrugged and moved away. One of the two range-dressed men standing on Moran's right came along the bar and nudged Moran's elbow as he raised his glass to drink. Beer splashed down Moran's jacket. He set down the glass and turned to face the newcomer, expecting an apology, but the man merely glared pugnaciously.

'What's sticking in your craw?' Moran demanded.

'Soldiers are a damned nuisance,' the man

replied, his jaw jutting angrily. 'Why the hell are they stuck out there at the fort? There's no Indian trouble now. They are a waste of public money. They don't spend much in town, and raise hell every chance they get. When they are in town on Saturdays it ain't safe for women and children to be on the street. Why aren't they employed on something worthwhile, like hunting down the bad men we're plagued by? That's what I'd like to know.'

'What's your name, mister?' Moran demanded.

'I'm Deke Sloan. I own the Lazy S cattle ranch, and I'm in town at this time of the day to report the loss of some steers instead of attending to my business.'

'Do you suspect that soldiers stole your cattle, Sloan?' Moran kept his tone steady.

'Nothing would surprise me,' replied Sloan sneeringly. 'I think soldiers should be banned from coming within a mile of Cactusville. My daughter came into town for the dance in Bennett's barn last Saturday and was manhandled by a drunken soldier.'

'Did you make a complaint to the commanding officer at the fort?'

'That would have been a complete waste of time. I've got a description of the man, and when I meet up with him, he'll be sorry for what he did. I'll take a horse whip to him.'

'It would be far better to complain to the fort and have him dealt with by the military authorities,' Moran said.

Sloan turned away. 'It would be a waste of my

time,' he said. 'Others have complained about similar incidents, and nothing has ever been done about them.'

Moran drained his glass, glanced at Bessemer, and nodded towards the batwings. Bessemer took the hint and led the way out of the saloon. They paused on the boardwalk. Moran looked around the unlovely street. He saw the town marshal standing in the doorway of the law office.

'You take a look around town, Sergeant,' Moran suggested. 'Keep your eyes open for Clark. If you do see him then arrest him and bring him to the law office.'

'Yes, sir.' Bessemer saluted and made himself scarce.

Moran went to the law office. Bowtell, the marshal, was staring fixedly at the dust in the street. He seemed miles away. Moran spoke to him twice before he looked up.

'How'd you get on at the fort?' Bowtell asked. He turned, entered the office, and Moran followed him into the welcome shade.

'I've made a start on what I came here to do. Did you catch any of the bank robbers?'

'That'll be the day!' Bowtell shook his head and sighed. 'The posse is still out looking. I can use my time to better purpose back here.'

'My job is to locate a trooper named Clark. Did you know him before he was jailed?'

'I had some trouble with him.'

'Have you seen him since he deserted?'

Bowtell frowned. 'I would have arrested him if I saw him. I wouldn't want him running around loose in town after he went loco over Laura Tipple.'

'Tell me about it,' Moran invited.

'I've got a better idea. I have to go to the bank and get some statements about the robbery. Why don't you head for the general store and talk to Seth Tipple? He'll tell you all you want to know. Then come back to me later and we can go on from there.'

Moran agreed and left the office. He walked to the store and entered. A tall beanpole of a man, white-haired and thin, was talking to three female customers. His apron was two sizes too large. He looked haggard and overcome by problems. He looked up as Moran entered, and his craggy face showed relief as he left the women and came to Moran.

'Can I help you, mister?' he demanded.

'There are three women ahead of me,' Moran pointed out, smiling, 'and I wouldn't want to be accused of pushing in.'

'Take no notice of them. They won't want serving until they've run out of gab. That's my wife in the yellow dress, and she can't get enough of local gossip, God bless her.'

'I'm Provost Captain Moran, Mr Tipple, and my job is to locate and arrest Trooper Clark, who escaped from the fort guardhouse a short time ago. I've heard that he was seeing your daughter before the trouble started, and I'd like to speak to her to learn the background of what went on.'

27

'I'm sorry, I can't help you,' Tipple replied. 'When Clark was arrested, I sent my daughter to Austin to stay with my brother, and she ain't coming back, ever. Clark pestered her nigh to death when she turned him down, and I was certain that if he got to her he would kill her.'

'It was that bad, huh?'

'You wouldn't believe it.' Tipple shook his head. 'I hope you get him quick, and if you shoot him dead trying to take him then I'll feel pretty good about it.'

Moran looked into Tipple's eyes, saw worry in their depths, and knew the storekeeper was not joking.

'I heard that Clark was seen around town after he busted out of the fort,' Moran said. 'Being a local man, have you any idea where he might hide out?'

Tipple nodded slowly. 'There's one man – Stark Shorten – owns a horse ranch north-east of town; sells remounts to the fort. He's a hard case, but Clark seemed to hit it off with him, and I reckon you might learn something about Clark's whereabouts if you catch up with Shorten. But walk softly around him. If you go out to his place to see him, he might start shooting before you can ask any questions. He's like that. He reminds me of a man who is waiting for a lawman to tap him on the shoulder.'

'Thanks for the information.' Moran turned to depart. 'I'll see Shorten right now.'

'Rather you than me,' Tipple replied softly.

Sergeant Bessemer was coming along the sidewalk when Moran emerged from the store. Bessemer paused at Moran's side, shaking his head in reply to Moran's enquiring gaze.

'No sign of Clark,' he reported. 'I reckon he hit the trail for other parts as soon as he got clear of the fort. What do we do now, Captain?'

'We keep on plugging away at finding him. I've got a lead I need to check out. I heard that Clark and a man called Shorten were good and friendly before Clark went into the guardhouse. Do you know where Shorten's horse ranch is?'

'I sure do. Let's get our horses and head north-east.'

They collected their horses from the hitch rail in front of the saloon and rode along the street. Bessemer inched ahead, turned into an alley beside the bank, and then crossed a back lot. When they came to a trail, Bessemer turned left and they headed north.

'We'll ride into Shorten's yard if we keep on along this trail,' Bessemer said. 'It's about twelve miles. Shorten is the kind of man nobody but a fool would tangle with. He ain't got a sense of humour; shoots first and asks questions later. Don't attempt to creep up on him. You'll get a slug if he spots you.'

'Don't gab so much, Sergeant. I've got things to think about while I'm riding. Just tell me when we get to Shorten's place.'

'Yes, sir. I'll ride a few yards ahead, shall I?'

Moran nodded and Bessemer pulled ahead. Moran began to muse over the information he had gained. But it was early days, and there was nothing cut and dried about any part of the situation. Apart from Clark, there was the unknown man who could not resist shooting at the fort from Spyglass Hill; he had killed Lieutenant Sandwell, left no clues to the incident and, Moran sensed, there was no earthly chance of finding any.

They rode surrounded by absolute silence, and were discomfited by the blazing sun. The range was illimitable. Moran, despite his thoughts, was constantly alert, ready to plunge into action at the first sign of trouble. He was faintly surprised when Bessemer interrupted his musing.

'Shorten's spread is just over the next ridge, Captain. And begging your pardon, sir, I don't think it would be wise to ride in and confront him. You might have to kill him before you can question him.'

'Does he know you by sight?'

'We know each other, sir, but he wouldn't let a small detail like that change his intention. He'd shoot me in the back without a pang of conscience.'

'We'll ride in openly. If he caught either of us sneaking around he'd have every right to start shooting. I'm beginning to look forward to confronting him – a man who would shoot down innocent callers without batting an eyelid. Let's get on and do our duty.'

Bessemer urged his horse forward and they ascended the rise before them. From the crest, they saw a small ranch consisting of a shack, barn, and two large corrals, one of which contained more than twenty horses. There was no sign of humans. The front door of the shack was closed, as was the door of the barn, and deep silence was spread over the place like a heavy blanket.

'Looks like there's no one home,' Bessemer observed.

'We'll take a look from closer in,' Moran decided. 'Just remember we're here to seek information. No shooting unless you're forced to defend yourself.'

Bessemer nodded and led the way down the slope. They reached the gate and crossed the yard. Moran saw that a pane of glass was missing from the window beside the door of the shack, and a tingle of some sixth sense made its presence felt in his breast. He reined in twenty feet from the shack, and his voice echoed when he called stridently.

'Hello, the shack. I've come to talk to Stark Shorten. I'm Provost Captain Moran on duty from the fort.'

The echoes of his voice were still sounding when a shot was fired through the broken window. A bullet struck the ground beside Moran's horse and whined menacingly across the yard.

'Get the hell outta my yard. You ain't got no business here. My next shot will let daylight through you. Get out while the going is good.'

'I'm here on Army business, and I'll talk to you before I leave. There's no two ways about that, Shorten, so show yourself and cut out the tough act.'

The rifle was fired again, and Moran heard the slug pass his right ear within a couple of inches. Moments passed in a deathly silence, and then

31

Moran spoke again.

'OK, you've made your point. Come out now and we'll get down to business. I've got other things to do today and you're wasting my time.'

The silence dragged on, and then a voice called out.

'And what'll you do if I don't come out?'

'I'll come in there and drag you out. Don't mess with the Army, Shorten; you can't beat the cavalry. I can put twenty men around here; or fifty if I have to. What are you getting so het up over? I only want to talk.'

'You're sure giving him some good advice, Captain,' Bessemer observed.

'Let's hope he'll accept it,' Moran replied.

A moment later, the door of the shack was opened and a big man stepped into the doorway, holding a rifle which immediately covered Moran. Shorten was at least three inches over six feet and built like an ox. His battered black Stetson was pushed to the back of his head, revealing a mass of curly brown hair. His expression was like that of a she-bear with cubs to protect – face contorted, eyes filled with passion.

'OK, so you don't scare easy,' Shorten snarled. 'What do you want with me? I've got a busy day myself – the horses in my corral have to be delivered to the fort today. So get to it. I'm listening.'

'Are you gonna drive twenty horses all by your lonesome?' Moran demanded.

'So you looked over my place before showing yourself, huh?' Shorten grinned.

'It's good military practice,' Moran replied.

'Well, I'll tell you. I've got a couple of men riding with me, and they are in this shack right now, covering you with their guns. So don't go getting any fancy ideas about pulling a fast one on me.'

'You talk like a man with a guilty conscience,' Moran observed. 'I want to talk to you about Trooper Clark. You knew him well before he was jailed, and when he deserted and broke out of the guard house at the fort, he didn't have any friends he could turn to except you. Have you seen him since his escape?'

'You're wasting your time if you've come all this way to ask fool questions like that,' Shorten said. 'Who I see and talk to is my business.'

'Answer my question.' Moran's voice cut like a whip.

Shorten's grin widened. 'Mister, you're saying all the wrong things. I ain't wearing one of your fancy blue uniforms so don't come into my yard and talk to me like I should jump to your tune. I ain't seen Clark since before he went into the guardhouse, and that's an end to it.'

Moran watched Shorten turn and re-enter the shack. Bessemer laughed and Moran frowned at him.

'We've wasted a handful of time this morning,' Bessemer observed.

Moran smiled. 'Is that what you think? Tell me, where is Shorten going today?'

'You heard him. He's taking some horses to the fort.'

'And we'll be there waiting for him.' Moran turned his horse and started for the gate. He had a tiny shiver of anticipation between his shoulder blades because Shorten was behind him. 'Let's get out of here,' he said sharply, and touched spurs to his horse; urging it into a faster gait.

Bessemer increased his pace, and drew level with Moran as they passed through the gateway. The sound of a shot sounded behind them and Bessemer uttered a cry and crumpled in his saddle before pitching sideways to the ground. Moran thrust home his spurs and his horse leapt forward. As he hauled on his reins to seek cover, a second shot rang out and he felt the tug of a bullet against his tied-down holster. His mount ran into a gully and they were lost to sight to Shorten and his two-man crew. Moran sprang out of his saddle, pulled his carbine out of its saddle boot, and ran back to the edge of his cover.

He saw Bessemer stretched out in the dust just this side of the gate. The sergeant was unmoving, and Moran could see blood seeping out of a wound in his back. Another shot came from the shack, struck the ground within an inch of Moran's face and sprayed dust into his eyes. He ducked, wiped his eyes, and then got up and ran into the yard, weaving from side to side. Shots came at him but he kept moving, his carbine in his left hand and his pistol cocked and ready in his right hand. . . .

THREE

A puff of gun smoke erupted from the broken window and Moran fired at it without seeming to take aim. A bullet whined by his head but he ignored it, and he fired two more slugs through the window while moving for cover at the right hand side of the shack. A man came out of the shack at a run, triggering a stream of lead at Moran, who dropped to one knee and sent a quick shot in reply.

The man fell face down in the dust and did not move again. Moran got up and ran for the window of the shack. He saw movement there and tossed a slug into it. He saw a quick movement and glimpsed a figure falling to the floor. He reached the wall of the shack beside the window and paused, breath searing his throat and shoulders heaving. Sweat ran down his face.

'Hold your fire, Soldier-boy,' Shorten yelled from inside. 'My two men are down and out of it. They started the shooting against my orders. I ain't such a fool I'd tangle with the military while I'm working for them.'

'Come out of the shack with your hands up,' Moran rasped.

He waited until Shorten emerged from the building with his hands in the air. Moran approached him from behind and searched him for weapons. There was a set grin on Shorten's slack lips.

'You sure are a heller, Captain,' he observed. 'Now you better tell me how I'm gonna get those horses to the fort, huh?'

'You won't be taking them – at least not today. I'm gonna put you in the fort guardhouse and then send for the town marshal to come and pick you up. You'll face several charges, and one of them will be for murder. My sergeant looks like he's dead, so head over there to him and we'll check his condition.'

'I didn't fire a shot in that little spat. My two men got out of hand, and I reckon they're both dead. You could have waited until they helped me drive the horses into the fort before shooting them.'

Moran nudged Shorten's shoulder with the muzzle of his rifle. 'Cut the gab and get moving,' he ordered.

They went to where Bessemer was stretched out, and Moran could see that the sergeant was dead.

'Pack him on his horse and then we'll take a look at your two men.'

Moran watched Shorten closely as the sergeant's body was hoisted on the back of his mount. Shorten led the horse to the front of the shack. They checked the other two men, found both were dead, and Moran made Shorten get two horses and load the cadavers. They set out for the fort, Shorten leading the three bodies while Moran rode at his back with his right hand resting on the butt of his holstered pistol. Shorten was passive during the ride, but when they reached the fort, he stirred in his saddle and gazed at Moran.

'You'd better think over what you're gonna say about what happened at my place,' he said. 'I didn't shoot the sergeant, and you've got my two men to blame for what happened. That's the easy way to handle it. If you're gonna accuse me of murder then you better think again. There ain't no evidence to prove I did it, and I'll walk free at the trial, so why make needless trouble?'

'I'll tell the truth about what happened,' Moran retorted. 'There was no need for any shooting at the shack. I told you what I wanted – to talk about Clark – and you pushed for gun play and three men are dead as a result. As for you not firing a shot in that fracas, I saw you shooting at me and the sergeant, and that fact will go into my statement.'

'You won't make that stick against me.' Shorten grinned. 'I got friends in the fort, and in town. You'll be facing a mess of trouble if you charge me with anything.'

Moran leaned towards Shorten's horse and struck it on the rump with the flat of his hand. The animal jumped forward and ran into the fort, and the dead men went along as their horses dragged at their reins.

The sentry on the veranda in front of the headquarters building turned out the guard when he saw dead men in Moran's party, and a sergeant and three troopers appeared as Moran stepped down from his saddle. Sergeant Major Craven emerged from his office and saluted Moran.

'You've had some trouble, sir,' he observed. He gazed at Shorten, sitting slumped and surly in his saddle. 'Is he under arrest, Captain?'

'There are several charges against him,' Moran said, 'and murder is one of them.'

Craven's eyes turned cold when he recognized Sergeant Bessemer face down across his saddle. He looked into Moran's face, and his lips barely moved when he spoke.

'Did Shorten kill him, sir?'

'I didn't see the incident.' Moran spoke through his teeth.

'But Shorten is under arrest on suspicion?'

Moran nodded. Craven turned to the sergeant of the guard. 'Sergeant Grimes, take the prisoner to the guardhouse and put him behind bars. I'll see that Marshal Bowtell is informed that we have a civilian prisoner.'

Two troopers hauled Shorten out of his saddle and led him protesting vociferously to the guardhouse. He scuffled with his escort at the door of the prison, and yelled at the watching Moran.

'I want to see Mallory the lawyer. Get him out here fast.'

'Is Major Harmon back from town?' Moran asked Craven.

'Not yet, Captain. The Major usually makes a day

38

of it when he leaves the fort.'

'I'll write out a report of my visit to Shorten's place, and then I'll return to town. I'll see the marshal about Shorten. I think we'd better keep him here while I'm making my investigation. I'll see Shorten's lawyer, too.'

'Right, sir. By the way, I've moved you into different quarters – a room that is not overlooked by Spyglass Hill.'

'I appreciate that, Sergeant-Major.'

'I'll send for your orderly and he'll show you to your new quarters.' Craven turned to the nearest trooper and rapped out an order that sent him off at the double, to return within moments with Trooper Myhill following.

The new quarters were on the other side of the housing block, and Moran was pleased to see his uniform laid out and ready to wear.

'Is there anything I can get you before you go into town, sir?' Myhill asked.

Moran shook his head. He changed into his uniform and stamped into his boots.

'Take my mount to the lines, have a fresh horse saddled for me, and I'll ride into town. It's time I started looking around for Clark. I've got a hunch that he is still around here, and I need him behind bars.'

He sat reading his copy of the summary of evidence until Myhill returned, and left his quarters to find a deep-bodied grey waiting for him. He mounted and left the fort, his mind busy as he cantered to Cactusville. There were one or two points in the sheets of evidence that needed checking out, and he was keen to get to grips with the problems. Someone in the fort had aided Clark's escape, and he had to start asking questions.

FOUR

When he reached town, Moran went to the law office, and found Art Bowtell at his desk, reading a newspaper. The Marshal leaned back in his seat when Moran walked in, a quizzical look on his rugged face.

'What happened out at Shorten's ranch?' Bowtell demanded. 'A range hand dropped in here an hour ago and reported hearing shooting coming from the direction of Shorten's place. He went in to look around and found blood in the dust of the yard and Shorten gone. I knew you were heading out that way earlier, so I reckoned you had something to do with it. What happened?'

Moran explained, and Bowtell shook his head.

'I was afraid that might be the answer,' he mused. 'Shorten is an oddball. But I didn't think he was crooked.'

'What makes you think he's crooked?'

'Why else would he start shooting when you dropped in on him? Did you find any sign of Clark out there?'

'I didn't get the chance to look, but I'll go out there again and check around. I want to talk to Mallory the lawyer.'

'He's the first man Shorten would ask for. Watch out for Mallory; he's sharp as a new pin.'

'Aren't all lawyers?' Moran countered. 'Do you know where Major Harmon goes to when he's in town?'

'I ain't seen him around, but I can tell you where he'll be – the hotel. The widow Mrs Grant runs it. Her husband, Charles Grant, was shot in the back more than a year ago.'

'Did you get his killer?'

'No. He was shot by someone using a rifle from a great distance.'

'Like Lieutenant Sandwell, huh? Shot on the parade ground in the fort from someone on Spyglass Hill.' Moran nodded. 'I'll be getting around to that particular incident when I've handled the assignment that brought me here.'

'You're gonna be real busy from now on,' Bowtell retorted.

Moran left the law office and looked around the street. He caught a glimpse of a blue uniform down by the bank and watched Major Harmon walk along the sidewalk to a doorway almost next to the saloon. Moran headed in the same direction, and halted in front of the door by which Harmon had entered the building. There was a brass plate beside the door. On it was a name – Vernon Mallory – and underneath an inscription: ATTORNEY AT LAW.

When Moran put his hand on the door to open it, someone inside the building grasped the handle and turned it. Moran stepped back. The door opened and Major Harmon emerged. Harmon halted in shock at the sight of Moran. His expression changed and a spark of emotion came to his sharp features. It was gone in an instant, but not before Moran had noted it. Moran was surprised when the word guilt blossomed in his mind, and he wondered what the Major could be guilty of.

'Hello, Captain. You're doing your investigation, I suppose. What have you discovered so far?'

'Today's activities will be on your desk first thing in the morning, Major. When I write a daily report, I always include an assessment of what I've learned and how it fits into the investigation. That assessment comes to me as a result of constructing a mental picture of what I am doing and thinking. That's the way I work, and it usually leads me to the man or men I want to arrest. But I'll tell you this. I went to talk to a horse rancher this morning who is a close friend of Clark, and shooting broke out. Sergeant Bessemer was killed, as were the two drovers who worked for the horse trader.'

Harmon's face turned pale. 'Who is the horse trader?' he demanded.

'A man named Shorten. Tipple said he'd heard that Clark and Shorten were friends. I heard that Clark was still in the area, so I thought Shorten was a good bet to question.'

'What happened to Shorten?'

'I arrested him and lodged him in the guardhouse at the fort. I've got some more questions to put to him. I'll charge him with Sergeant Bessemer's murder, and there will be other charges.'

'Why did Shorten attack you?' Harmon's face was expressionless but he was tense and seemed worried.

'That's one of the questions I want Shorten to answer.'

'And you are here now to see Mallory, are you?'

'That's right.'

'Mallory is out at the moment so you'll have to come back later. I've just asked for him and was told he won't be around until this evening. Did you get anything from Shorten about why he attacked you?'

'Nothing yet, but it is early days. You seem concerned about Shorten.'

'I am. He was due to deliver twenty remounts to the fort today. I've had lots of dealings with him over the past few years, and he's always been straight with me. We need those remounts, and we need them now. That's what concerns me.'

'Send a detail from the fort to pick them up.'

'I shall have to.' Harmon turned away, and Moran saluted him.

Moran walked along the boardwalk. When he glanced over his shoulder, he saw Major Harmon going back the way he had come. Moran halted, and watched Harmon enter the hotel. After a few moments, Moran went in the same direction, entered the hotel, and strode into the restaurant. He saw Major Harmon seated at a table with a middle-aged man who was well dressed in good quality clothes and looked to be a man of business. Harmon saw Moran, and said something to his companion, who turned his head and studied Moran for some moments before resuming his meal. Harmon left the long room. Moran sat at a table by the door and waited for a waitress to approach him.

He ordered food, and ate hungrily when it arrived. He was aware that he was under close scrutiny by the man Harmon had spoken to, and when the waitress came to him with a plate of apple pie, Moran asked her the identity of the watching man. The girl looked around, frowning.

'Do you mean the smartly dressed man?' she asked.

Moran nodded.

'That's Bruno Reinhardt, the sutler at the fort. Don't you know him?'

'I arrived at the fort this morning,' Moran replied. 'I haven't met anyone there except Major Harmon.'

Moran finished his meal, and sat considering the case. Nothing added up, but it was early days yet. He was about to get up and leave when Reinhardt arose from his table and came to the exit. He was tall and heavily built, but didn't seem to be carrying much fat. He was wearing a light blue suit and a string tie. His face was smooth, his lips thin, a mere slash under his nose. His blue eyes were sharp and alert, like a horse trader's. He paused beside Moran, who looked up at him. Reinhardt was smiling. He made a slight bow.

'Please excuse me, Captain, I should like to introduce myself. I am Bruno Reinhardt, the sutler at the fort. Major Harmon told me you're a military policeman, here to capture the deserter Clark. I hope you get him. He stole a quantity of merchandise from me before he deserted.'

'I saw nothing about that in the summary of evidence, Mr Reinhardt. If you have a claim against Clark then see me at the fort and I'll include it.'

'Thank you, Captain. I'll see you later.' Reinhardt turned to leave but Moran spoke and stopped him.

'Is there anything more you can tell me about Clark?' he asked.

'I don't think he left the area after he deserted.'

'What makes you think that?'

'I thought I saw him here in town one night last week.'

'Was it a definite sighting or could you have been mistaken?'

'It was him all right. He was with another man, and when he spoke I recognized his voice.'

'Did you report the sighting to Major Harmon?'

'I try not to become involved with the daily working of the fort, Captain. But I've reported it to you now, and that should be sufficient.'

'Can you tell me who the other man was? He could lead me to Clark.'

'It was dark and I didn't get a look at him. I wish now I had told the Major about it.'

'And so do I! They might have caught Clark, and Bessemer might still be alive.'

'I'm sorry about the sergeant. He was a fine soldier.' Reinhardt lifted a forefinger to his hat and departed.

Moran sat for some moments, digesting the news about the sighting. He filed the fact away in the back of his mind as the waitress approached with the bill for his meal. He took the bill to the desk in the lobby where a young woman was seated, paid it and walked out to the street. When he paused to look around, he heard a sound like the crack of a bullwhip, and hurled himself off the sidewalk into the dust of the street. He had been shot at too many times in the past not to recognize the sound of a closely passing bullet, and his gun was in his hand as he looked around for gun smoke. The echoes of the shot faded slowly, hanging on the breeze, and no one on the street seemed to notice the disturbance.

A second shot was fired, and a spurt of dust sprang up a couple of inches from Moran's left elbow. He judged that it was a long shot by the sound of the report, and he sprang up, turned and dashed into the doorway of the hotel before the gunman could reload. As he ducked into cover, a third shot sounded; a bullet ploughed into the woodwork surrounding the door and splinters flew.

Moran moved to the front window of the building and peered out cautiously, aware that the bullets could only have been fired from almost across the street. He listened to the fading echoes while his keen gaze swept the roofs of the buildings opposite, and he lifted his pistol when he caught a fleeting glimpse of a figure peering around the wooden façade of the butcher's shop. His finger tightened on the trigger but he held his fire – the figure had vanished.

He went outside the hotel and ran across the street; entered an alley to gain the back lot. He turned and scanned the rooftops again, and saw a figure carrying a rifle scrambling hurriedly along the apex of the roof of the bank. He ran along the back lot, content to follow the figure until it jumped onto a flat part of the roof, which was out of sight to Moran. He waited, but the figure did not reappear.

Moran continued to wait and moments fled by. He suddenly got the idea that the figure had reached his point of leaving the roof area. He ran along the nearest alley to the street and emerged beside the bank, his gun still in his hand. He went into the bank; saw a man dressed in a town suit standing beside an office door, conversing with a smaller man, and confronted them. Both men stared at him, their expressions changing when they saw the drawn gun in his hand.

'Which of you is the banker?' Moran demanded.

The smaller man pointed to his companion, who said, simultaneously, 'I'm Henry Maxwell, the banker.'

'Is there a way up to your roof from inside here?' Moran said. 'I was shot at by someone from up there.'

'That's impossible.' Maxwell shook his head. He

was short and fleshy, with a florid face and dark eyes. 'The trap door leading to the roof is in the cupboard in my office and I've been here for the past hour. No one could get to the roof unnoticed.'

'Can you prove that?' Moran said.

'Prove it?' Anger showed in Maxwell's face and he seemed to swell with indignation. 'Who are you to come rushing in here waving a gun and demanding to search the bank?'

'I'm Captain Moran, Military Provost. I'm in the area to investigate a deserter and various other crimes that have been committed by troops.'

'I have a witness,' Maxwell said. He glanced at his companion. 'This is Vernon Mallory, the lawyer. He's been in my office with me since I got back from my meal at the hotel. Perhaps you'll take his word that no one has been up to our roof in the past hour.'

Moran looked at Mallory, smartly dressed and of handsome appearance; looking every inch a lawyer. His blue eyes were fearless as he gazed at Moran.

'Mr Maxwell told you the truth, Captain,' said Mallory as if he were standing in front of a judge in a courtroom. 'You can take my word for that, and there's no one in this town who would doubt anything I utter.'

'I need to go onto your roof and check it out for myself,' Moran said to Maxwell.

'This way,' Maxwell replied, and led the way into his office.

A desk was set beside the window overlooking the street and a large safe, as tall as a man and four times as wide, was set into the wall on the right, with a cupboard door on its left. Maxwell went to the cupboard and opened it. He motioned for Moran to enter.

'There's the ladder. Unbolt the trapdoor at the top. You can climb through the trap and get out on the roof. Just don't ask me to accompany you – I don't have a head for heights.'

Moran entered and went swiftly up the ladder. He drew back a couple of iron bolts and threw the trap back on its hinges. It crashed back on the roof and Moran climbed the last few rungs and stepped out on to the roof. His gun covered the area as he turned to survey it, and he started in shock when he saw a man sitting on the roof just yards from where he stood.

'Help me,' the man called. 'I was in the dress shop, which my wife owns, and heard feet thudding overhead. I came up to investigate, and my left foot plunged through a rotten piece of board. My right leg twisted awkwardly as I went down, and I think I've done some serious damage to it. The pain is pretty bad, and I can't move.'

'Have you got a gun on you?' Moran demanded.

'I never carry a gun.'

'What would you have done if you'd found a man up here, one who had fired several shots at me as I emerged from the hotel?'

'So there was someone up here. Can you get my leg out of this hole?'

Moran holstered his pistol and approached the man, took him under the arms, and lifted him. The man cried out in agony and motioned for Moran to desist. Moran noted that as he raised the man, the piece of wood that had broken under his weight was pulled up by the movement of the leg and had jammed itself against his boot. He lowered the man to his former position, snapped the piece of wood, and lifted the man again. The foot came out of the jagged hole without causing more trouble, and Moran sat the man on the roof.

'Who are you and where did you come out on the roof?' Moran asked. He noted that the man was ashen-faced; tall and heavy, and too old to be crawling around on a roof.

'I'm Dan Archer. Like I said, my wife owns the dress shop.'

'Did you see anyone up here?'

'No. My foot went through the roof before I had time to look around. Can you get me down from here? I can't use my right leg.'

'Wait a minute.' Moran went back to the trap door and called to Maxwell. 'There's a man up here. Says his name is Dan Archer. Do you know him?'

Maxwell was standing at the foot of the ladder, his face upturned to Moran. 'Of course I know Dan. He owns the dress shop his wife runs. He's also the town mayor. What's he doing up there?'

'We'll get him down before asking questions,' Moran replied. 'Get a man to ascend the ladder and help me to get Archer down. He's going to need a doctor. He's done himself a serious injury.'

Maxwell called the teller, a younger man, who ascended the ladder until he was close to the trap door, and Moran eased Archer through the aperture. Between them they moved Archer to Maxwell's office, and the teller was sent to fetch the town doctor.

Moran stood over Archer, studying the man, wondering if his explanation of events was true. He contained his impatience and waited for the doctor to arrive. But the town marshal put in an appearance, attracted by the shooting, and Moran stood back, aware that his time would come.

FIVE

Bowtell bullied Archer, but could not shake his story. When Bowtell suggested that Archer was telling lies, the town mayor became indignant and began to shout.

'I don't need this aggravation right now,' he declared. 'Get the hell out of here, Bowtell, and see me later. The only man I need to see right now is Doc Arnott. Where in hell has he got to? I'm suffering here. I want something to kill the pain.'

'You've got no one to blame for what happened but yourself,' said Maxwell unsympathetically. 'You didn't have to go climbing on my roof. I could have told you there was a rotten board up there but I didn't think you would be fool enough to go up there and walk around.'

Bowtell took his leave when the doctor arrived, departing swiftly, as if he had just remembered something important which needed attention. Arnott examined Archer's injuries, put a bandage on the lacerated flesh of the leg and then picked up his medical bag.

'That's all I can do for you here,' Arnott said. 'I'll get some men to carry you over to my office.'

Moran grew impatient and left the bank. He walked to the dress shop and entered. A tall, slim woman of some thirty-five years emerged from a room at the back of the shop. She was smartly dressed, and looked out of place in a cow town like Cactusville. Her long black hair framed her face, and when she smiled it was as if the sun had come out unexpectedly on a rainy day. Her dark eyes gleamed as she regarded Moran.

'I'm Corinne Archer. Do you need a new dress, Captain?'

Moran smiled. 'It's been a long time since I wore a dress,' he replied. 'That was in the days when I was a baby. Folks used to put a boy in a dress until he started running around. I'm here on a different matter, Mrs Archer. I'm Captain Slade Moran, military police, and I'm in this area to deal with soldiers who have broken the law. A few minutes ago I met your husband on the roof of the bank. He put his foot through a rotten board and injured his leg.'

'I've been wondering where Dan had got to,' she said. 'We heard the sound of someone moving around on the roof, and Dan insisted on checking it out. Where is he now? Is he seriously hurt?' She went to the door. 'I must go to him.'

'Not at the moment,' Moran said. 'He's in the bank having his leg dressed by the doctor. Tell me about the noise up on the roof. Was it a man moving around?'

'It was, and it's not the first time I've heard those noises. They've been going on for weeks. At first I thought it was someone fixing the roof, but when I made enquiries, no one seemed to know anything about it. I complained to Dan several times. He put it down to my nerves and didn't take me seriously. But he was here in the shop today and heard the noises too. That's why he went up on the roof.'

'He should have called the town marshal.'

'That's what I told him, but he wouldn't listen to me.'

Moran shrugged, as if to say that was how it was with men. He turned to leave, his mind filled with conjecture about a man on the roof of the bank. He stood on the sidewalk considering the problem. Had the man gone up to the roof merely to shoot at someone down at street level? And how had he disappeared so quickly? Archer had gone up to the roof as soon as he heard movements above his head, and Moran had not wasted time getting to the scene, but the unknown man had disappeared.

Moran went back to the bank. Maxwell was alone in his office, and he looked up impatiently from a ledger he was scrutinizing. He sighed heavily and threw down his pen.

'What is it now, Captain?' he demanded.

Moran advanced to the desk and stood over the banker. 'I don't like the tone in your voice, Maxwell,' he said harshly. 'It may be inconvenient for you to have people interfering with your daily life, but that's the way it goes when the law has been broken. You may not know it but I have the power to enter any place in the course of my investigations and question anyone who might know something that might help me to ferret out the truth. What I want to do right now is go out on your roof again and take a closer look around. Have you any objection to that?'

'No!' Maxwell got hurriedly to his feet and came around the desk. 'Please forgive my show of impatience. It's been a bad day so far. Did you know that the bank was robbed this morning?'

'I heard about it.'

'Four men walked in just after opening time and cleaned out the big safe – and if that was not enough, you turned up saying a man was on my roof and had shot at you.'

'That's why I want to carry out another check up there.' Moran followed Maxwell to the cupboard. He paused as he was about to pass the banker and gazed into the man's eyes. 'I have a feeling about this,' he said. 'Someone could be hiding up there permanently. His movements have been heard on more than one occasion lately.'

'That's preposterous! No one could hide up there. There's nothing up there to hide in or under. We don't store things up there because of the fire risk.'

'I'll soon find out.' Moran began to climb the ladder. 'I may not come back down this way so don't worry if I do find something interesting up there and it leads me away.'

'I can think of better things to do than crawl around a rooftop,' Maxwell declared.

Moran went up the ladder to the trap door, opened it, and climbed out onto the roof. Looking around, he could see that Maxwell had told the truth about there being nothing lying around which could be used as cover. He walked around the area, watching where he placed his feet, and finished on the edge overlooking an alley. He judged the distance to the building across the alley to be about five feet.

He walked along the roof to the alley on the other side of the bank, tested it, and decided it was solid enough to take his weight on the run. Moving back in the direction of the trap, he started to run, and launched himself over the alley. He landed safely on the other side with a couple of feet to spare, and subjected the roof to a search, but soon changed his mind about searching. There was absolutely nothing on the roofs that could be used as cover.

He returned to the roof of the bank and gazed over the front edge at the street. His mind was busy. Questions arose from his subconscious mind, all clamouring to be answered. Who had taken shots at him? Someone who wanted him dead? But who knew him? And what had Dan Archer been doing on the roof of the bank?

Moran was getting a feeling that there was a set-up here in Cactusville which involved a faction of the community making a play for illegal profits. He decided to sit back and watch points. If his hunch was right then someone was certain to give himself away.

He used his experience to gain headway, and had some leads to work on. First on his list was Shorten, whose actions at the horse ranch were highly suspect, and Sergeant Bessemer had died as a result. So there had to be connections between Shorten – and whom? Dan Archer? If Archer had not stepped on a piece of faulty board, no one would have known he had been on the roof. Had the town mayor fired the shots from up there? If so, where was his rifle? There had been no sign of a weapon when Moran found him. Had he thrown it off the roof when he became trapped by his leg?

Moran cut off his thoughts. They were leading him into a morass of conjecture. He descended to the bank, took his leave of Maxwell, and went outside, heading for the back lot to check for a weapon along the rear of the bank. He found nothing.

He heard a noise from the alley he had used, and saw Art Bowtell emerging. The town marshal came towards him. Moran considered him as he halted. He was grinning, and Moran thought that he would not be in a light mood if he had failed to get the men who robbed the bank that morning.

'Looking for anything in particular?' Bowtell asked.

'I'm checking for the gun that was fired at me across the street from the bank.' Moran sighed and relaxed. 'I guess I made a mistake. But I was certain I was shot at from the roof of the bank.'

'Dan Archer was up there when you looked,' Bowtell mused.

'Do you think he took those shots at me?' Moran demanded.

'Hell, no! I'm just looking at the facts.'

'Archer didn't have a gun with him. He told me how he came to be on the roof, and his wife bore out his statement. Do you know what I think? You've got a bad set-up around here. There's a bunch of dishonest men working together to extract what they can from the community. So who do you know who is crooked?'

'You think I know who's doing what around here?'

'You know the community, and there must be some men inside of town limits who don't work regularly but have money to spend. Point me in their direction and I'll try to expose them.'

'You must be getting desperate if you're ready to try a stunt like that.' Bowtell shook his head. 'I wouldn't attempt it. I'd be dead before I started asking questions.'

'But you know who they are,' Moran insisted.

'A couple of names spring to mind.' Bowtell shook his head slowly. 'I'm not inclined to mention them because they might cloud the issue.'

'Are there any soldiers on your list? Is Clark still around here?'

'I ain't set eyes on him, and that's a fact, and there's been no talk about him since he busted out of the fort. The soldiers have a run-in with the townsmen at times, but it's nothing serious.'

'You're not doing your job properly if you can't pinpoint the hard cases around town.' Moran set his jaw pugnaciously. 'Are you trying to hide something, Marshal?'

Bowtell allowed a tight grin to pass across his face, but his eyes were hard and unfriendly. 'I'll overlook that, seeing who you are,' he grated. 'It sounds as if you're getting a mite desperate. OK, I'll give you a name and we'll see what you can make of it. Bart Swain works in the saloon as a gambler, and he's slippery as an eel. I've always reckoned he was up to no good around here, but I've never caught him out, so see what you can do. Now that I'm thinking about him, I remember your deserter, Clark, was friendly with him.'

'Thanks.'

Moran turned and went to the saloon, leaving Bowtell to stare after him. He pushed through the batwings and went to the bar. The saloon was not busy, and there was no sign of Bart Swain. Moran asked for beer and, as he paid the bartender, asked, 'What time does Swain start his job?'

'Around seven. Feeling lucky, are you?'

'I can usually hold my own,' Moran replied. He glanced at his pocket watch, saw the time was just after six p.m., and took his beer to a table where he could watch the ebb and flow of business through the batwings.

The saloon began to fill as the evening drew on. Several cowboys pushed through the batwings, cheerful, brash and noisy. They bellied up to the bar and called for drinks. Townsmen began to put in an appearance. The batwings banged and creaked incessantly. Then Bart Swain entered from the rear of the saloon, easily recognized for the gambler he was. Moran studied the black-suited figure. Bart Swain was no more than thirty years old, tall and good-looking. He was gaunt-faced, as if his occupation and its attendant dangers were too stress-filled to be handled casually. He wore a grey Stetson to relieve the funereal colour of his suit. His eyes were brown and unblinking beneath his hat brim.

Swain sat down at a large table in the centre of the saloon, and the 'tender came hurrying over from behind the bar with a bottle of whiskey and a glass. The 'tender spoke cheerfully, but Swain did not break his hard expression or acknowledge the 'tender's presence. The 'tender went back behind the bar and Moran, anticipating a general drift towards the gambler's table, moved in first and dropped into a seat opposite Swain.

'This table is used for private games and by invitation,' Swain said in a clipped tone. 'I don't know you, Captain, and I don't want to.'

'I'm not here to play poker,' Moran replied harshly. 'I'm a military policeman sent into this area to investigate the actions and activities of certain troopers stationed at Fort Tipton. I have heard that you were friendly with Trooper Clark, who escaped from the guardhouse and killed a fellow trooper during his escape.'

'Did you say Clark?' Swain's eyes took on a wary expression.

'I doubt there is anything wrong with your

hearing,' Moran retorted. 'I did say Clark.'

'I don't recall the name off-hand. So many faces show up around this table and I can't remember them all.' Swain reached inside his jacket and produced a pocket watch. He glanced at it and then replaced it in his pocket. Moran caught a glimpse of a shoulder holster and the butt of a small-calibre gun before the lapel of the jacket closed in to conceal them.

'Am I holding up your scheduled game?' Moran asked.

'You could have picked a more convenient time. But I have nothing to say that would interest you. You'll be wasting your time trying to push this line of your investigation with me.'

'I'll be the best judge of that. Just answer my questions. I have a job to do, and I'll do it come hell or high water. There are two ways we can handle this, and it's up to you which way we do it. You can co-operate and be helpful or you can handle it the way you are doing, and if I'm not satisfied with your attitude and information, I can make life very difficult for you. I have the power to arrest you on suspicion of withholding information, and I'll take you into the local law office and hold you until I get what I want. Do you understand?

'So what was your question?'

'Do you remember Clark? I heard that you and he were friends before his arrest.'

'Who told you that?'

'I'll ask the questions and you answer them;

nothing more.'

Swain's dark eyes seemed to smoulder and his thin lips pulled into an almost invisible line. The fingers of his right hand twitched as if he wanted to pull his hidden gun. Moran watched him silently, outwardly casual, but tense and ready to flow into action. Swain heaved a sigh and tried to relax.

'I knew Clark,' he said without seeming to move his lips, and his hard gaze did not leave Moran's face. 'I wouldn't call it friendship. He played poker at times, and seemed to be above the usual run of soldiers. He was interesting.'

'Have you seen him since his escape from the fort?'

'No. If he had the sense I thought he had then he would be far away by now.'

'Did he have other friends in town?'

'We didn't talk on a personal level. What he did and who he knew was of no interest to me.'

Moran knew he would make no progress with Swain. He stood up and prepared to leave, but paused and looked into the gambler's inscrutable eyes.

'That wasn't so bad, was it?' he said. 'I may need to talk to you again, Swain, depending on what I learn from other sources of information.'

Swain ignored Moran and turned his head to look at a group of men standing at the bar. 'I'm ready to play poker now,' he called.

Moran turned away as four men left the bar and hurried to the gambler's table. He bought another beer and sat down close to a small raised stage at the rear end of the saloon. A man was seated at a piano beside the stage, and he began to play the instrument. A woman appeared from a back room and came to stand beside the piano. She began to sing, and Moran leaned back in his seat and gave her his full attention while his mind ticked over the points of his investigation.

The woman was tall and had a good figure that showed to advantage in an off-the-shoulder blue dress. She was beautiful, her blue eyes bright and glowing with vivacity. Moran got the feeling that she was singing to him personally, and he noticed that her gaze favoured him among the men present in the saloon. When she finished singing, she surprised him by approaching his table, waving and smiling to her audience.

'Good evening, Captain,' she greeted. 'I haven't seen you in here before. Are you new at the fort?'

Moran got to his feet. 'I arrived this morning. Would you like to sit down?'

'Yes. Thank you.' She paused while he drew out a seat for her, and flashed him a quick smile as she sat down.

'Would you like something to drink?' he invited.

'Not at the moment, thank you. If you arrived at the fort this morning then I assume that you are Captain Moran, the military policeman.'

'News travels fast in this town,' he observed.

He could tell by her manner that she had something on her mind, and he was concerned. His first glance at her had struck an unfamiliar chord in his mind and he was instantly attracted to her. The sound of her voice appealed to him, and he gazed into her eyes and felt concerned by the sorrow that filled them.

'I knew two weeks ago that you were coming here, and I've been waiting for your arrival. I'm Ruth Sandwell, Captain. My brother was Lieutenant Sandwell, who was murdered in the fort three weeks ago.'

Moran leaned forward in his seat, suddenly very interested. 'I'm pleased to meet you, Miss Sandwell, and I'm truly sorry about your brother. One of my duties is to look into his death. If there is anything you can tell me that will help my investigation then I'll be happy to listen to you.'

'We can't talk here,' she replied swiftly. 'It's too dangerous for me. No one here knows who I am. I'm calling myself Ruth Kelling. I have a room at the hotel. Could you come there to see me after I finish my stint here? In fact, I could pretend to have a headache after my next song and leave early.'

'I'll meet you when and where it would be most convenient for you,' he declared.

'Thank you, Captain. You'll find me in room nine at the hotel.'

She smiled at him and arose abruptly. He watched her cross the stage and enter a room, and then he finished his drink and left the saloon. He was elated by the turn of events. Ruth Sandwell obviously knew something of the circumstances of her brother's death, and he controlled his impatience and waited in the shadows of the alley next to the saloon. . . .

It was some twenty minutes later when Ruth emerged from the saloon, and she was accompanied by a tall man who was well dressed and talked in a loud voice. They passed closely by Moran; the man in full conversational flow.

'Are you sure you're gonna be all right, Ruth?' he said. 'I can get Doc Arnott to come to the hotel and look you over. It's no trouble.'

'It's just a headache, Chuck,' she replied. 'I think it's the spotlight you have shining on me when I'm on stage. It's so bright, and it is centred right between my eyes.'

'We got to let the customers see you, Ruth. You're going over big, and that means money. You take care now, you hear? We've got something good going here.'

'Just get that spotlight adjusted so it doesn't blind me when I'm singing,' she told him.

Moran followed them as far as the alley beside the hotel, and got a good look at Chuck as the man escorted Ruth into the hotel. The stranger was a big, wide-shouldered, handsome man with fair curly hair and an expansive smile. He must be the saloon owner, Moran thought. He waited in the shadows of the alley, and ten minutes later, Chuck emerged and went back along the sidewalk in the direction of the saloon.

Ruth quickly opened the door when Moran knocked on the centre panel of room nine. He stepped inside and she closed the door. Her face was serious now; eyes dull with an inner pain. He glanced around the room. There was a single bed by the window, a couple of easy chairs, and little else except a small table with two chairs at opposite ends. Moran sat down at the table. Ruth opened a cupboard and produced two glasses and a bottle of whiskey.

'My father is a Colonel in Washington,' she explained as she poured whiskey into the glasses. 'He was against my coming here, but I insisted. He found out about you coming here and arranged for me to be on hand when you arrived. Do you know what happened to my brother?'

'Only that he was killed while on the parade ground by someone outside the fort shooting from a nearby place called Spyglass Hill. Tell me about your brother. I intend looking into the circumstances of his death when I can get the time.'

'Frank was sent here by our father because there is something seriously wrong at the fort. He reported that the troopers were close to mutiny some weeks ago. Discipline was slack, the troopers were causing trouble here in town, and everyone was beginning to call the fort by a nick name – Fort Hatred. Colonel Davis was posted. They put it around that he was ill and unable to do his duty, but he was suspected of dereliction of duty. A large quantity of rations, guns and ammunition had disappeared from the store, and have not been traced.'

Moran listened intently. But Ruth did not have much to tell him. Her brother had written reports to his father but merely mentioned the crimes being committed without supplying names of the people involved. Ruth's voice quivered as she explained that Lieutenant Sandwell had been killed before he could expose the guilty men.

'There's not a lot to go on,' Moran mused when Ruth fell silent. 'I did not know the extent of the trouble.' He saw the expression which crossed her face and hastened to reassure her. 'But I expect to make an impression on the situation. There will be loose talk around the fort and I'll glean facts from it. I'll keep in touch with you and you'll be able to report to your father. But don't tell anyone your real identity. There are some bad men around town as well as in the fort, and the fact that you are a woman would not stop them from silencing you to save themselves.'

She nodded, and from her expression Moran was able to see the extent of her anxiety. He got to his feet and reached for his hat, his mind dilating with unusual sympathy.

'We'll have to be careful about how and where we meet.' He wanted to pass the thought to her that she was not alone, that he would help her where he could because he found her different and he wanted to get to know her better.

She nodded. 'I have struck up a friendship with Major Harmon, thinking that he has most opportunity of knowing what is going on. But he is close-mouthed and defensive. He seems to have a lot on his mind, but that might be down to the fact that he has taken over command at the fort and is now responsible for what happens next.'

'If I have anything to tell you, I'll drop in at the saloon so it looks as if our meeting is above board. You can be sure I shall be watched, and anyone I talk to will be under grave suspicion by the men I seek.'

'I'm not unduly worried about the risks I shall be taking,' she replied. 'My brother died in the execution of his duty and I want to bring the circumstances to light, no matter the cost.'

Moran shook her hand and departed, carrying with him a picture of her soulful eyes and the expressed determination that inwardly drove her.

He left the hotel and stepped into the darkened alley beside it, but he heard nothing but quickly sensed a presence behind him. He turned quickly, reaching for his holstered gun and raising his left arm defensively. The shapeless darkness seemed to leap at him, and he tried to duck the upraised pistol that descended to strike him. When the blow landed it was as if all the stars in the firmament collided inside his head. His half-drawn gun fell from his suddenly limp hand; shrouding shadows blacker than the night enveloped him. He was not aware of falling to the ground. . . .

SIX

The town marshal, making his evening round of the town, checking doors and inspecting businesses, stumbled over Moran's unconscious body and cursed under his breath when his entire body weight crashed onto his left knee. He sprawled in the alley, pushing his face against the hard ground before rolling on to his back. He drew his gun before reaching out to check what had caused his downfall, and the yellow kerchief around Moran's neck gave him his first intimation that the senseless man was a soldier. He felt for a match, struck it, and looked down into Moran's stiff face.

Bowtell got to his feet and lifted Moran bodily; carried him into the hotel and put him down on a couch. Charles Grant, the owner of the hotel, was at the reception desk, and watched Bowtell without making any movement to assist. Grant was short and rotund, smooth-faced and weak-chinned. His blue eyes were screwed up as if he had trouble seeing normally.

'Is he dead?' Grant demanded. 'If he is, you can take him out of here pretty damn quick.'

'He's not dead,' Bowtell replied. 'Go fetch Doc Arnott.'

'Not me. I don't want to get involved. He's the new captain that showed up at the fort today, huh? He's just like the rest of those officers – useless.'

Bowtell controlled his temper. 'Just watch him until I get back,' he rapped. 'I'll fetch the doc.'

He hurried out to the street and rapped on the doctor's door, which was opened by Arnott's wife, a small woman with a neat figure and a careworn face; white hair which was sparse at the crown.

'Is the doc in, Mary? I've got an Army officer at the hotel. Someone clouted him with the barrel of a pistol.'

An inner door was opened and Arnott appeared, carrying his medical bag. He was short and fleshy, and nodded affably when he saw Bowtell.

'I knew I was wanted as soon as I heard your knock, Marshal,' he said.

They left the house and went back to the hotel. On the way Bowtell gave the doctor some details, and then they entered the hotel. Arnott examined Moran, who was still unconscious, and his face was expressionless as he reached into his bag and produced a small bottle. He removed the stopper and held the bottle under Moran's nose. Moran was breathing deeply and evenly. For some tense moments he did not respond to the doctor's ministrations and Bowtell thrust out his bottom lip when

71

there was no reaction. Then a shudder ran through Moran's frame and his head moved spasmodically. His eyes opened a crack and his lips moved silently.

'Take it easy, Captain,' Arnott advised, 'you've had a heavy blow to the head. Just lie quiet until I've finished my examination.'

Moran glanced around and animation seeped into his expression when he saw Bowtell in the background.

The lawman said, 'I was doing my round of the town and fell over you in the alley next door. Did you see who hit you?'

'No,' Moran mumbled, and closed his eyes wearily.

'You shouldn't go to sleep after a blow to the head,' Arnott said. 'Are you staying in town?'

'I certainly don't feel up to riding back to the fort,' said Moran hesitantly.

'You'd better come with me and I'll let you sleep in a cell in the jail until tomorrow morning,' said Bowtell.

Moran agreed, and Bowtell helped him to his feet. The doctor departed and Moran moved unsteadily. Bowtell escorted him along the street to the jail, opened an empty cell, and Moran flopped on the bunk and lay motionless, his body quiescent but his aching head churning with questions to which he could find no answers. He fell asleep eventually, and did not stir until the sun next morning was well over the horizon. When he opened his eyes and came back to reality, his head felt as if it had been split open by an axe.

He sat quietly in the cell, recovering slowly from the murderous blow that had rendered him unconscious. He recalled nothing about the incident and finally gave up trying to remember.

Bowtell came through from the front office, his face careworn, eyes peering from their wrinkled sockets.

'How you feeling this morning, Captain? I didn't expect to see you sitting up. You must have a thick skull. Do you have any idea who struck you?'

Moran refrained from shaking his head. The pounding beat of the agony tormenting him was almost too much to bear.

'I didn't see anything,' he replied.

'I reckon someone is out to get you. Could it have been Clark getting worried about your presence in town?'

Moran pushed himself to his feet, and grabbed the bars of the cell to remain upright. He closed his eyes while a bout of dizziness assailed him. When the movement ceased, he picked up his hat and set it gingerly on his head.

'I need some breakfast and coffee,' he said. 'Then I'll start looking for the men giving me trouble.'

He went to the diner, which was crowded, and shared a table with Bruno Reinhardt, the sutler from the fort. Reinhardt took one look at Moran's face, saw a blood stain on his forehead and uttered an ejaculation.

'You look like you got in the way of a stampede, Captain,' he observed. 'What happened to you?'

'It was a bad dream that came true,' Moran replied. 'In my line of business it happens more often than I care to think about.'

He felt easier after eating breakfast and drinking two cups of coffee. He sat back in the turmoil of the busy mealtime and ran his thoughts over what had happened to him so far. He had been shot at before he reached the fort, and then someone had put two slugs through the windows of his quarters. He had been shot at on Main Street, and considered the incident on the roof of the bank without finding a glimmer of enlightenment. Ruth Sandwell had added another dimension to his investigation, and her arrival into his calculations brought a whole host of questions into being, a number of them personal. Ruth seemed to have entered his mind like a spirit, and he felt possessed. He found it almost impossible to nail down his conjectures, and answer all the questions passing through his mind. He should have known exactly what had gone on around the fort before his arrival, but the end result of his musing was strangely missing.

He went back to the law office, wondering what had happened to his horse.

'We've got a barn out back,' Bowtell told him. 'I put your horse in there, and your blanket roll is in the cell you used.'

Bowtell collected the blanket roll and accompanied Moran out to the barn. He saddled Moran's horse and tied the blanket roll to the cantle.

'That's all I can do for you, Captain. You're own your own now. If I were in your boots, I'd head back to fort and hit the sack for a couple of days. You look so bad I've got a feeling that I should escort you.'

'I'll be OK now.' Moran led his horse outside and swung into the saddle. The movement set his head spinning and he sat for some moments until it resettled.

Bowtell stood watching him, arms akimbo. Moran finally shook his reins and gripped his horse with his knees as the animal went forward. He headed back to the fort.

It did not take him long to sense that he was being followed. He stayed off the trail and left the town, regaining the trail to the fort when he judged he was out of sight of prying eyes. He rode at a lope and did not look around. His head ached and he closed his eyes from time to time, but he had a tingling sensation between his shoulder blades, and could not ignore it. He rode into a stand of trees, halted, and drew his pistol, his chin on his chest. Several minutes later two men came into view, riding at the pace he had employed, and one of them was gripping a pistol in his right hand. The sight of the drawn gun warned Moran that he had trouble on his hands, and perversely, he welcomed it.

The two riders approached the stand of trees. They were looking around intently at the ground, searching for tracks.

'I don't see him anywhere,' one of them observed. 'Do you think he's got wise to us?'

'I've done better than that,' Moran rasped, kneeing his horse out of cover. 'I've got you dead to rights.'

The pair reined in quickly and the man holding the gun flipped it up to cover Moran, who squeezed off a shot. The bullet took the man in the chest. The crash of the shot echoed and Moran clenched his teeth as his head protested at the noise. He covered the second man, who was frozen in shock in his saddle until the first man slid sideways out of his saddle and thumped on the ground.

'Get rid of your gun,' Moran directed, 'and be careful how you handle it. I'm hair-triggered.'

The man plucked his pistol out of its holster and let it fall to the ground. Moran steadied himself by placing his left hand on the saddle horn and stiffening his elbow. The man raised his hands shoulder high and remained motionless. He was rough-looking, wearing range clothes. His Stetson had seen better days. It was pushed to the back of his head and his brown hair showed, lank and long. His face was lined with shock and his eyes took on a haunted expression.

'Have you got a name?' Moran demanded.

'Dick Coe. What's the idea attacking us?'

Moran laughed. 'Is that the best you can do?' he demanded. He glanced at the dead man. 'Who's he?'

'Lobo Watson; we ride for the Lazy S. We came into town to report a bunch of steers were rustled from the ranch last night.'

'So why did Watson try to shoot me as soon as he

saw me?'

'I guess you startled him when you came out of the trees. You could have been a rustler.'

'I don't like your story.' Moran waggled his gun. 'Get down and put Watson across his horse. Then we'll go back to town and see what the marshal makes of you.'

Coe protested strongly as he dismounted. He threw the dead man across his saddle and then remounted, and protested all the way back to Cactusville. Moran was pleased with the incident. Watson had tried to kill him, and that indicated involvement. They rode into town and proceeded to the law office. Moran had his pistol in his right hand and was fully alert. As they reined up at a hitch rail, the law office door opened and Bowtell appeared.

'It looks like you found some more trouble,' Bowtell observed.

Moran explained before dismounting, and as he eased himself out of the saddle, Bowtell drew his gun and covered Coe.

'You did a good job,' Bowtell said. 'I know this man's face. There's a wanted notice in the office. He's Dick Coe – wanted for bank robbery. Why was he after you?'

'That's what I need to find out,' Moran told him.

'Let's get him into the office.' Bowtell looked around. Several townsmen were coming towards the office, drawn by the sight of a man face down across his horse.

Moran slid off his horse and walked unsteadily into the office behind Coe and the town marshal. Coe was pushed into a chair before the desk and Bowtell stood over him.

'So what's the story, Coe? What did you and Watson want with Captain Moran?' Bowtell demanded.

'They gave me some story about riding for the Lazy S ranch,' Moran said. 'They were coming into town to report a rustling loss to you, but when I first saw them they were riding in the opposite direction to town, and Watson was holding his gun. When I confronted them Watson tried to shoot me.'

'So they were lying!' Bowtell holstered his gun, grasped Coe's shoulders and dragged him upright; slapped him several times across the face before thrusting him back into the chair. 'Let's have a taste of the truth now,' he rasped. 'There's been a posse out for you and your gang all day. So what's going on? Why were you after the Captain?'

Coe shook his head. Blood dribbled from a corner of his mouth. Moran watched him intently, his mind flitting over the salient points he had already gleaned, but there was nothing solid to work on, and he controlled his impatience and let Bowtell handle the questioning.

'Your gang has been in the county for some time,' Bowtell continued. 'Where have you been hiding out? You'd better come clean and tell me what I want to know. You killed a man in the bank this morning, and a townsman was shot dead as you left town.

Feeling is running high around here, and as soon as word of your arrest gets out there'll be a lynch mob outside my door, yelling for me to hand you over to them. So you'd better make up your mind now and talk.'

'You got the wrong men,' Coe replied. 'I've never robbed a bank in my life, and we weren't in on the one in this town.' He looked into Moran's eyes with unblinking gaze. 'If you tell the truth about what happened out of town when we met, then you'll admit that I didn't do anything to break the law. It was Watson holding his gun, and he tried to shoot you. But I don't know why. He never said a thing about attacking an Army officer.'

'Perhaps he had a thing about the military,' Moran said. 'Lieutenant Sandwell was killed on the parade ground in the fort by an unknown killer.'

'I don't know anything about that.' Coe shook his head.

'And is it true about you and Watson riding for the Lazy S ranch?' Moran persisted. 'Were you on your way to town to report the loss of a herd?'

'That was a lie, but Watson was a dyed in the wool liar. He wouldn't recognize the truth if it blew into his face.'

'So what have you been doing around here when you weren't robbing banks?' Bowtell asked.

'We did some work for a horse rancher named Shorten, collecting horses to be sold to the military at the fort.'

'When did you last see Shorten?' Moran asked.

'We finished the round up yesterday and he paid us off.'

'Where did you spend last night?' Bowtell cut in.

'Here in town. We had some money in our pockets and had us a good time.'

'Where did you sleep?'

'We hit the sack in the livery barn, and lit out before sun up. Watson had a thing about hanging around folks. He was afraid someone might recognize him.'

'And you met up with some of your pards this morning and came back to rob the bank here in town,' Bowtell said. 'You better level with us, Coe, if you want to keep your neck out of a noose.'

'That's all I can tell you,' said Coe, shaking his head.

'I'll put him in a cell for a couple of days,' Bowtell said. 'He'll change his story plenty when he hears a mob out on the street yelling for his neck. Come on, Coe, empty your pockets on the desk and then I'll get you settled behind bars.'

'I'll drop in later,' Moran said. 'I've got some items to check on before I go back to the fort.'

He left the office, mounted his horse, and rode back along the street, his mind seething with conjecture.

When he saw Ruth Sandwell emerging from the hotel he caught up with her. She looked around at the sound of his voice and smiled a greeting.

'I was thinking about you, Captain. I'm pleased to see you.' She paused and a shadow crossed her face.

'You've had some trouble since last night,' she observed. 'I see bloodstains on your forehead, and you look as if you've been attacked.'

Moran stepped down from his saddle and hitched the animal to a rail in front of the boardwalk.

'Are you feeling all right?' Concern sounded in her voice. 'What happened to you?' He explained and she put a hand on his arm. 'I've recalled some things my brother told me before he was killed, and you should know of them before you go any further. You look all in, Captain. Could you do with a coffee? We need to sit down and talk and I'll show you the notebook my brother kept on what he had learned at the fort.'

Moran nodded and the girl turned and re-entered the hotel. She walked into the dining room and he followed her closely. His head had picked up a relentless throbbing that threatened to turn into a crippling headache, and he was relieved to be able to sit down and relax. When they'd had coffee, Ruth leaned her elbows on the table and gazed at him intently.

'I don't think you are well enough to do your duty today,' she observed. 'You should return to the fort and rest. You could be suffering concussion. Your eyes indicate that your brain is not functioning normally.'

'I'll manage,' he told her. 'What can you tell me? I'm still at the beginning of my investigation, and there is little I can accomplish without more knowledge to help push things along.'

He was keenly aware of how beautiful she looked in the light of day. Her eyes were gleaming with excitement and hope. He caught a faint tang of an intangible perfume about her as she moved in her seat, and it remained in his nostrils, lifting him out of his despair. He placed his elbows on the table and supported his chin, for his head seemed too heavy for his neck to support.

He was recalling the briefing he had received at headquarters before setting out in this investigation. Nothing had been mentioned beyond the fact that Trooper Clark had escaped from the fort, having committed murder during his escape. Now he was becoming aware that a great deal more had been going on in the background, and he suspected that someone in higher authority was concealing important facts.

'My brother said he learned that the Army is being robbed systematically. The sutler, Bruno Reinhardt, is at the heart of it, and Colonel Davis was involved. That was why he was removed from command. The Army is trying to limit the scandal. But my brother was murdered, and I assume the whole business is still proceeding as if nothing had gone amiss.'

'I've met Reinhardt, and I'll investigate him.' Moran suppressed a sigh. 'I heard Colonel Davis was retired because of ill health. I'll make some enquiries at headquarters about him, and you can bet that I'll get exactly what I ask for. Now I'd like to see that notebook your brother kept.'

'It's in my room. I'll fetch it. Will you wait here?'

Moran nodded and she left him. He thought about Reinhardt, and questions reared up in his mind. Major Harmon loomed up out of the grey area, with a big question mark over his head, and Moran wondered where he fitted into the business. The Major was handling the remounts, and the man contracted to gather the horses was Shorten. Moran suspected that a strong link existed between the two, and he was impatient to get into his stride and dig into the facts.

Ruth returned and sat down. She was holding a notebook, and opened it; flicked through some of the pages before glancing up at Moran.

'Listen to this,' she said. 'Frank says here that he happened to overhear part of a conversation between Reinhardt and Maxwell, the banker. Frank made friends with Cora Maxwell, the banker's daughter, and he was visiting her home when Reinhardt arrived to talk to Maxwell. Cora drew Frank into another room, and he overheard much of what Reinhardt said before Cora moved him out of earshot of the conversation.'

'May I read it for myself?' Moran asked.

Ruth handed him the notebook and he perused the closely written words. Frank Sandwell had a good hand, and Moran felt a strand of excitement unwind in his mind as he read on.

Reinhardt was angry with Maxwell, who became angry in turn but was on the defensive. It seems that

Maxwell was reluctant to complete his preparations for the forthcoming bank robbery, and there was trouble with Shorten, who was trying to push up the prices he charged for the horses he was delivering to the fort. The departure of Colonel Davis made life more difficult for everyone involved, so greater effort had to be made.

Ruth reached forward and touched the notebook. 'That's the most important entry Frank made, and just a bit further on he had this to say.' She turned a couple of pages and paused for a moment, and when she started reading a quiver sounded in her voice.

I think I've been discovered. I've been asking too many questions and someone has become suspicious. I was duty officer yesterday, and when I was checking the stables a knife was thrown at me but missed.

She looked up and met Moran's hard gaze. 'He goes on to say he was unable to get a look at the man, but saw him briefly as he disappeared, and is trying to identify him.'

'Did he say anything more before he was killed?' Moran looked into her eyes and saw the over-brightness of unshed tears in their depths. He had to take a tight rein on his emotions in order to remain objective. That was the effect she was having upon him.

Ruth shook her head and did not speak.

'This gives a good picture of what was going on,

and it clears some of the mystery of your brother's death,' Moran mused. 'When I first heard that he had been killed I imagined he had upset someone in town, but now it looks as if he was killed by someone in the fort.'

'I hope you can uncover the activities of the guilty men,' she said, 'and I'd like to know the identity of Frank's killer.'

'Can I take this notebook with me?' Moran picked it up. 'I can stir up a hornets' nest with it.'

'Certainly.' She smiled wanly. 'But be careful you don't get stung in the process.'

He nodded and put the notebook into a pocket. 'I must go now, but I'll be back to talk to you again.'

She smiled, and he arose and departed, suddenly finding himself with a great deal to do. He went for his horse, intending to ride out to Shorten's horse ranch. His mind picked over what he had learned from the notebook like a buzzard ripping its prey. His head had eased somewhat by the time he neared Shorten's place, and as he rode towards the gateway, he heard the sound of several horses approaching from the opposite direction. He rode swiftly into cover, and did not reveal his presence when he saw the blue uniforms of cavalry. A troop of soldiers from the fort rode into the ranch and opened the corral gate. They hazed the horses into the open and headed them in the direction of the fort. Moran waited until they had gone from sight before leaving cover to enter the ranch yard.

He entered the shack and looked around intently,

wanting records of Shorten's dealings with Major Harmon. He found nothing, and guessed that a man like Shorten would not keep anything that might tie him into any deal. He made a mental note to check with Harmon about recent remount transactions.

The sound of hoofs outside alerted him and he drew his pistol before moving to the window overlooking the yard. Three riders were coming towards the shack, and Moran stepped into the doorway as they drew within gunshot range. Two of the men were in their twenties, range-dressed and hard-eyed. The third rider was better dressed, a tall, lean man who looked as if he could take care of himself in any situation. He was older, and when he spoke, the tone of his voice gave Moran the impression that he was accustomed to giving orders.

The three men slowed their pace at the sight of Moran. Two of the men dropped their hands to the butts of their holstered guns and eased back slightly. The third man came on determinedly, undaunted by Moran's ready gun.

'Who are you and what are you doing here?' he asked in a rough tone.

'I'm Captain Moran, military provost. I'm investigating some trouble at the fort. What's your name?'

'Deke Yelding. I own the Lazy S ranch. One of my men was out this way earlier and heard shooting, so I've come along to see what's doing. Where's Shorten?'

'He's taking some remounts to the fort. Are you a friend?'

'Hardly. He doesn't have friends. But I'm his neighbour, and I thought he might be in trouble.'

'There's a lot of trouble around here,' Moran said.

'Are you looking for the deserter, Clark?' Sloan asked.

'What makes you think of him?'

'I hear a new officer had turned up at the fort and was looking into the trouble there.'

Moran smiled. 'The folks around here seem to learn of events before they happen,' he mused. 'What's your interest in Clark?'

'No interest at all. They say he's a killer as well as a deserter, and he deserves to hang, if he's guilty.'

'We hang men only after they have been proved guilty, and all the evidence so far indicates that Clark did what has been claimed and laid against him.'

'If you're new to the fort then you won't know what's been going on,' Yelding said.

'If you know anything, I'd be very interested to hear what you have to say. What's on your mind, Yelding?'

One of the two men accompanying Sloan came forward, and as he passed behind the rancher, he drew his gun and cocked it. Before Moran could react, he found himself looking into the levelled weapon, and the face behind it was filled with deadly intent.

'Drop your gun and put your hands up,' the man grated, 'or you'll stop lead.'

Moran opened his fingers and his gun thudded on the ground.

The man grinned. 'I hear you've been looking around town for me,' he said.

'Who are you?' Moran demanded.

'Trooper Clark, the deserter everyone wants to see hanged; the man you came to Fort Hatred to arrest.'

SEVEN

Moran concealed his surprise. He shrugged. 'What's the point of this?' he demanded. 'Why did you stay around here after breaking out of the fort?'

'I'm not guilty of the charges and I had an idea that if I stuck around, I might prove it. Now I'm not so sure. I've been railroaded into this situation, and they'll kill me before I can get started.'

'I'm here to get at the truth of those charges against you, so if you've got anything to say then you're talking to the right man. Why don't you surrender to me and let me handle it? If you're innocent then I'd surely prove it.'

'No dice! I'm between a rock and a hard place, and there's no way out for me. I guess the only thing I can do is head for greener pastures and lose myself in the wide blue yonder.'

'Why don't you take the time to tell me exactly what happened at the fort and how you came to be saddled with murder? Name the men who want to see you found guilty of their crimes.'

'I can't risk losing. My life is at stake and my freedom is all I have. Why should you care about me? If I surrendered to you I'd wind up in the guard-house again, and next time there won't be any chance of escape.'

'I'm not a man to take evidence at face value,' Moran said. 'I make my decisions on the evidence I gather. I shall check on every line of evidence in this case, and if it does not stand up to investigation, I will eliminate it.'

Clark shook his head. 'I can't take the chance. They've got a hanging rope picked out for me at the fort, and I can feel it around my neck right now.'

'Give me a chance,' Moran said. 'I've already learned that something is bad at the fort that stinks to high heaven. In fact, I may be your only hope.'

Clark shook his head. 'I can't risk putting my life on the line. I guess it's time to cut my losses.'

Moran looked into Clark's eyes and saw what he thought was honesty. He realized that he had to consider the case from the aspect that Clark was innocent, and as he did so a different situation confronted him.

'You'll have to give me some proof that you are telling the truth,' he said. 'Is there anyone at the fort who can corroborate your claim to innocence?'

Clark shook his head slowly. 'They've set me up against the grindstone. I can see that now.'

'Then try to convince me that you are telling the truth. Give me facts that I can check. I have no desire to produce a miscarriage of justice.'

Yelding, who had remained silent during Clark's insistence of innocence, spoke in a warning tone.

'There's dust over in the direction of the fort. It must be a patrol, and it's coming this way.'

Clark turned instantly and ran to his horse. He mounted, whirled the animal, and in a few moments he was lost to sight in the brush. Moran made an instinctive move towards his pistol, which was lying at his feet, but Yelding covered him with a gun and warned him to stand still.

'You have the right idea of not taking the evidence against Clark at face value,' Yelding said. 'There is a lot wrong at the fort and the guilty men are running free. If you go for Clark and arrest him, you'll be aiding the bad men, for they'll see Clark hanged out of hand and all suspicion will die with him.'

'I'm in no position yet to make up my mind about who is guilty,' Moran mused. 'If Clark would trust me and give himself up it would make my job easier. But I can understand his reluctance. I won't pursue him now, but now I know he's still in this area, I shall have to take steps to apprehend him.'

He saw six troopers and a Corporal coming into the yard. Yelding holstered his gun.

'I'll be making tracks,' he said. 'You'd better keep your wits about you, Captain. The men who have framed Clark won't stand by and let you spoil their game.'

'I'm well aware of the dangers facing me,' Moran

replied. 'Before you go, tell me, do you employ two men called Coe and Watson?'

'Never heard of them.' Yelding touched his hat brim and rode away, followed by his rider. They disappeared around the shack. Moran picked up his pistol, dusted it off, and thrust it into his holster. The patrol came up and the Corporal saluted.

'I didn't expect to find you here, Captain,' he greeted. 'I'm Corporal Benteen.' He was tall in the saddle, bronzed, and looked fit and tough. 'My orders are to find you and check if you are OK.'

'Thank you, Corporal. I was about to return to the fort.'

'Were you having trouble with that rancher, sir?'

Moran shook his head. 'No, I was talking to him about local conditions.'

He swung into his saddle and rode towards the gate. Corporal Benteen came to his side.

'I have to make a trip to Cactusville, sir. Will you be OK to continue to the fort alone?'

Moran smiled. 'I'm quite capable of riding alone, Corporal. You can go about your duty.'

'Yes, sir, thank you, sir. It's all a matter of orders, Captain.' He saluted and turned away, calling to the patrol to follow him.

Moran was immersed in thought as he continued. None of his previous investigations had been easy, but this one looked as if it could turn into a humdinger. But he was looking at Clark's case in a different light as he pushed his mount into a lope and headed for the fort.

He went to the guard house, found Sergeant Coman on duty, and was taken to Shorten's cell. The horse rancher was sullen, and complained about his horses corralled on his spread. His expression changed when Moran told him the remounts had been collected and brought to the fort by a detail of troopers.

'When are you gonna turn me loose?' Shorten's voice rasped.

'It will be a long time before you see the outside again,' Moran told him. 'There's a charge of murder that could hang you, and even if you've got friends in high places they wouldn't be able to help you.'

'What do you mean, friends in high places?'

'You've been dealing with the fort for a long time, so I've been told.'

'Everything has been above board. Are you hinting I ain't on the level?'

'I haven't said a word about your dealings, so why are you protesting so strongly?'

Shorten shrugged. 'You're trying to pin a murder on me, so it's natural to think you'll hook on very other charge you can think of. But I didn't shoot your sergeant, and you can't prove I did.'

'Who handles the remounts when you bring them in?'

'Major Harmon and Jackson, the farrier sergeant, give them the once-over. They select the ones they want, I get paid for what they select, and I push the rejects back to my place.'

'Do you keep accounts of your dealings?'

'No need to. It is cash on the barrel-head, and everyone is satisfied. I've never had any complaints.'

Moran left Shorten moaning about his incarceration and went to the headquarters office. Sergeant-Major Craven called the two clerks to attention and saluted.

'Sergeant-Major, do you keep the remount ledger in the office?' Moran asked.

'No, sir. Major Harmon handles the remounts, and that ledger is on the shelf in his office.'

'Is the Major in the fort?'

'He hasn't returned from Cactusville yet, sir. Usually he doesn't get back until the early hours. Do you need that ledger now?'

'I shall have to check it as a matter of course. Get it for me, and I'll read it in my quarters.'

Craven fetched the remount ledger and Moran tucked it under his left arm.

'Did you make any progress in town, Captain?' Craven asked.

'Yes, I did. I saw Clark.'

'Clark?' Craven looked up at Moran to see if he was joking. 'Did you arrest him, sir?'

'I didn't get the chance. I talked to him some, and then a patrol showed up and Clark made a run for it.'

'Hard luck, Captain, but now we know for certain he's still around here, I'll order extra patrols out tomorrow to look for him.'

'No, don't do that. I have the feeling that I'll be able to get him without a lot of fuss when I want him.'

'I don't understand, Captain.'

'That makes two of us, but when I start throwing rocks into the water, the situation, after ripples, will become clear. Keep the news about Clark under your hat for now. OK?'

'Yes, sir.'

Moran departed. When he reached his quarters, he found his orderly, Myhill, waiting for him.

'Anything I can get you, Captain?'

'I'd like some information, Myhill. I need to know what was going on around the fort before my arrival.'

'I can't speak out of turn, sir.'

'I'll ask you a number of questions and I want you to answer them truthfully. I am the officer detailed to investigate the situation here, and as such I am able to question, and I expect to get truthful answers. If you don't answer truthfully you could incur severe penalties. Is that clear?'

'Yes, sir. But I don't know anything about what's been going on. There are always rumours on an Army post, but most of them are false.'

'Just answer my questions. Let's find out what you do know. If someone in the fort was running a racket involving the remounts, who do you think would be responsible?'

'Is that what you're looking for?' Myhill looked relieved, and drew a deep breath. He thought for a moment and then nodded. 'Shorten sells remounts to the fort, so he'd be involved, sir.'

'And who is likely to be in it on the military side?'

'Colonel Davis used to handle the remounts, but he was posted away. It was said he was unfit for duty.'

'And was he?'

'I don't know, sir.'

'You're an officer's orderly, so who were you taking care of before I arrived at the fort?'

'Lieutenant Sandwell. He was shot dead on the parade ground, Captain.'

'Someone wanted him dead. Have you got any thoughts on that?'

Myhill shook his head. 'Whoever is on the wrong side of the law doesn't go around with a placard pinned to his back telling all and sundry. I don't think you'll find a single man in the fort who would be willing to tell you what he knows.'

'And for the same reason you're refusing to answer questions. That's not good enough, Myhill. Someone has to stand up and be counted.'

'It would take a braver man than me to do that. My father told me before I joined the Army to keep my mouth shut and my eyes open; he knew a thing or two.'

'OK, we'll call this off for now, but I'm not finished yet. All I want is for someone who has been here during the past few months to tell me what he saw or heard and I'll do the rest. I'll give you time to think about what I've said, and I leave it to your conscience what you do.'

'What happens if I decide not to say anything, sir?'

'That will depend on how my investigation is going at the time.'

'Can I get you anything, sir?' Myhill was obviously relieved to change the subject.

'Not right now. I'll have a meal in town later. Right now I want to go through this remounts ledger.'

'I'll come back at six, sir,' Myhill said, and withdrew.

Moran settled down to read the ledger, and at first glance it seemed straightforward. He turned to the summary of evidence once more, looking at it from the point of view that Clark was innocent and some of the statements might have been made by a guilty party intent on heaping blame on him. He found several points which needed clarifying, and made notes to check later.

He sat musing over what he had read, and it was fairly obvious that he had to start using the usual tactics to make headway in the case, which meant starting a hunt for guilty men. It would be a longer, more searching method, but he was convinced that if there were guilty men trying to blame Clark for murder then he would be able to reveal it, given time.

Myhill reappeared at six. Moran dismissed him from duty for the evening, and was riding out of the fort an hour later. He went into Cactusville and led his horse into the stable, where an old man appeared, frail and unsteady on his feet.

'I'm John Barfield,' he announced. 'You're new around here, Captain? Are you replacing someone at the fort?'

'No, I'm here on other business,' Moran replied. 'Are there any soldiers in town this evening?'

'If there are then I doubt I would see them. They

won't pay my prices. There are a couple of barns on the back lot behind the saloon, and most soldiers put their mounts in them. I lose a lot of trade to Pete Marks, who runs the barns as stables.'

'I'll leave my horse until I'm ready to ride back to the fort later.' Moran tendered a silver coin but the stableman shook his head.

'I don't charge officers,' he said. 'If the place is closed when you come back, you can get in through the side door, and take your horse out the same way.'

'Thanks.' Moran watched Barfield lead his mount away, and went out to the street to look around the town.

Shadows were beginning to gather in the corners as shadows lengthened. A cooling breeze blew along the length of the street, and although the sky was filled with celestial fire, the day-long heat diminished appreciably. Moran went to the saloon and ordered a meal, which was served with a glass of beer that had been iced. He enjoyed the meal and relaxed with the beer, his mind gnawing at the facts he knew and seeking those which he had not yet discovered. He was jolted out of his thoughts by a figure that lurched against his table, and he looked up quickly to see Deke Yelding leaning over him.

'Evening, Captain,' Yelding greeted. 'Mind if I sit down for a couple of moments?'

'You look as if you've got something on your mind,' Moran commented. 'Sit down and ease your weight.'

Yelding dropped into the seat opposite and placed

a whiskey glass on the table. He glanced around the saloon, which was filling up, and then leaned across the table to speak in an undertone.

'That friend you met at Shorten's place earlier today asked me to come in and find you. He wants you to know that he's of a mind to trust you. So if you want to talk to him he'll meet up with you anywhere you care to see him. Just tell me the time and place and he'll be there, raring to go.'

'I'm glad to hear that.' Moran nodded. 'Let's say Shorten's ranch at noon tomorrow.'

Yelding grimaced. 'He says if he gets just one sniff of another soldier around, you'll never see him again.'

'That's fine. I'll be alone.'

Yelding nodded and slid out of his chair. He went to the bar and stood alone at the far corner. Moran finished his beer and departed. A stray thought slid into the forefront of his mind, and he was faintly surprised when it was followed by an image of Ruth Sandwell's face. He was thoughtful as he walked along to the hotel, hoping to see her, and his breathing quickened when he entered the hotel restaurant and saw her seated alone, eating a meal. He moved in and sat at a nearby table. She caught his movement and looked across, a smile coming instantly to her face.

'I was just thinking about you, Captain. Have you the time to talk later?'

'I was hoping to see you,' he admitted.

'Please join me,' she responded. 'I'm almost finished

here. Are you making any progress with your investigation?'

He joined her, sitting opposite. She continued with her meal and he took the opportunity to look at her. She was a beautiful woman, and he frowned when his thoughts seemed to slip out from under his control, despite his efforts to contain them.

'Do I pass scrutiny?' she asked quietly, and Moran realized she had caught him gazing at her.

'You passed earlier, with flying colours,' he replied. 'I'm looking at you now because I'm trying to assess your situation in this business.'

'How do you mean?'

'Your brother was shot and killed by someone who was afraid of being exposed. Now you are on the scene, and it is obvious what you're doing. The point is, the killer might feel so threatened by your presence he could make an attempt against your life.' He saw sudden fear spring into her eyes, but she controlled it quickly. 'I'm telling you this not to frighten you but to warn you to be very careful. The men involved in this trouble have no scruples when it comes to dealing with women. If you take my advice, you'll leave here and seek a safer place to stay. I doubt if you'll be able to do anything to help my investigation, and with you gone I won't have to worry about you.'

'I assure you that I have considered all the angles, and I should be lying if I said I'm not afraid. But my brother's killer must be brought to justice, and that knowledge will keep me here until I have seen the guilty man punished for what he did.'

'I'll make a special effort to expose him and bring him to justice.' Moran inhaled deeply, aware that an intangible frisson of her perfume was invading his sense of smell, and he breathed as if he could not get enough of it, the almost illusory fragrance invading his mind and freeing some of the deeply covered instincts he had been forced to bury below the surface when first he decided to follow the path his career had to take. For years he had led a lone existence, emotions lashed down under control. Initially he had been bothered when he'd had to kill in the execution of his duty, but he had become accustomed to dealing out death and bloodshed, and eased his conscience with the knowledge that he was doing his duty.

'I can't leave,' she said firmly, 'although I'd like to accept your advice and go. But I have to see justice done, no matter the cost, for I'd not be able to live with myself if I gave up now.'

He nodded. 'I understand, and I'll help you all I can. But I'm just idling at the moment. I want to be back at the fort just before sundown and be in the shadows watching for trouble as darkness falls.'

'That sounds like it will be highly dangerous.' She frowned. 'Do you have any help?'

'I like to work alone. I took a sergeant with me yesterday and he was killed.'

'So you're already attempting to unravel this mystery!'

'I never stop. It's that kind of a job. I usually

plunge in and muddle along until I get my teeth into some proof or other, and then try to arrest the guilty men. So far I've been lucky and managed to come out on top, but the cases seem to be getting harder and harder as I go on, and I expect my luck will eventually run out.'

Horror filtered into her eyes and she compressed her lips. He smiled to reassure her and prepared to leave.

'Do you have to go yet?' she asked.

'I'd like nothing better than to remain in your company but I have a very harsh mistress, and I'm completely under her thumb.'

'My brother had the same mistress, but he called it duty. I shall be worried about you until I see you again.'

'Don't worry on my account.' He smiled disarmingly. 'For the most part my job consists of waiting around, observing, which is all very boring, and when a case is successfully closed, the action is swift, and usually enacted with surprise on my side.'

'You make it sound so straightforward, but I know that isn't so.'

'I'll be in town again tomorrow afternoon, and I'll make a point of calling on you, if I may.'

'Please do,' she said eagerly, 'at any time.'

'I have an appointment at noon tomorrow, and if that goes well I'll be in town early in the afternoon.'

She looked up at him as he got to his feet, and opened her mouth to speak again, but he smiled and pressed a hand lightly on her shoulder.

'Until tomorrow,' he said gently, and turned away to leave without looking back.

A sigh escaped him as he walked along the side-walk in the direction of the stable.

He collected his horse and rode steadily back to the fort. By the time he entered the stockade, shadows were already gathering in the low places and night sentries were on duty. He handed over his horse to a groom and went directly to his quarters, staying there until full darkness arrived. When he judged it time to get moving, he removed his yellow neckerchief, checked his .45 Army Colt and put a handful of extra shells into a pocket.

He took care leaving his quarters, locking his door on the inside before opening the window and climb-ing out to the veranda. He stood in the shadows for some moments, allowing his eyes to become accus-tomed to the night. A deep silence lay over the fort. He saw shadows moving around – sentries on patrol, some guarding certain points. He moved around slowly, pausing frequently, probing the dense shadows.

There was a lighted window in the store at the end of the administration block, and he approached a window to sneak a look inside. Three men were standing at the desk by the door. He recognized Bruno Reinhardt, the fort sutler, and Marshal Bowtell, from Cactusville. The third man was a stranger to him, a sergeant with the insignia of a farrier on his sleeve.

Moran edged closer to the window, which was ajar.

He could hear their voices clearly, loud enough to enable him to understand what they were saying. He saw Reinhardt reach into the inside pocket of his coat and produce a thick wad of paper money, which he passed to Bowtell. The marshal grinned and thrust the wad into his breast pocket.

'I'm suspending our business until Captain Moran finishes his investigation,' Reinhardt said. 'We can't be too careful. I met him in town earlier, and he looks a tough character to me. I've heard of his reputation, and seeing him, I can believe every word. So I'm closing the business until he's gone.'

'What the hell!' Bowtell exclaimed. 'He's only one man, and I could soon put him out of the way if he proves to be troublesome.'

'That's the last thing we need, another murder on the scene,' said Reinhardt angrily. 'Just do as I say and we'll soon be back to hauling in money.'

'I've got used to the extra dough,' Bowtell protested. 'I've got expensive tastes, and I can't afford not collecting every month. I'll get rid of Moran if he bothers you.'

Moran leaned his right shoulder against the wall beside the window and pressed his ear closer to the pane of glass. He dimly heard the sound of a boot scraping on the hard ground behind him, and recoiled from the window, turning to meet what he knew was a threat, but before he could get into a position to defend himself, he was seized in an iron grip and the muzzle of a pistol was jammed painfully against his spine. He was faintly aware of a man at his

104

side, and then a heavy object struck him behind his right ear and lights exploded inside his skull as he pitched to the ground. . . .

EIGHT

Moran did not lose consciousness but the blow temporarily robbed him of his ability to move and think. He was dragged to his feet and supported, his toes dragging on the ground as he was taken in through the doorway of the big store room. His thoughts were chaotic and dense, as if his head had been filled with river mud. He was thrust to the ground and he lay blinking in the bright light, his head filled with throbbing pain. He heard voices but could make no sense of them. He raised his head, looked for faces, and saw Bowtell coming to check him. His hearing returned at that moment and the town marshal's voice hammered against his ears.

'What the hell have you done, Wilbur?' Bowtell demanded.

'This guy was sneaking around in the shadows,' a hoarse voice replied. 'I watched him look through several lighted windows, and when he peered through the end window here, I decided he was up to no good and gave him a whack with my gun.'

'You fool,' Bowtell replied. 'He's Captain Moran, and he gets paid to sneak around and catch anyone who is up to no good. He'll have your law badge off you for this.'

'I didn't know who he is. Heck, I was only doing my job. There are a lot of bad men in this fort, and I figured he was one of them.'

Bowtell helped Moran to his feet and brushed him down. Moran pushed him away and straightened. He staggered, and put a hand on Bowtell's shoulder for support. He looked at Reinhardt, who was gazing at him with a harsh expression on his face. The farrier sergeant was gazing at Moran, his fleshy face showing a mixture of despair and guilt.

Reinhardt pulled out a chair at the table. 'Sit him down here, Marshal,' he rapped. 'He looks like he could do with a stiff drink. I'll get a bottle.'

Bowtell helped Moran to the seat. Moran looked for the man who had hit him, and saw he was wearing a law star on his red shirt. His eyes were shifty. He looked like a bully to Moran, who was an expert at reading character at a glance and was seldom wrong. The deputy was still holding his pistol, and he grinned as he holstered it with a fast, experienced movement.

'Sorry, Captain,' he said in a leering voice. 'No hard feelings, huh?'

Moran did not reply. Reinhardt returned, carrying a bottle of whiskey and a glass. He poured a generous tot and set the glass before Moran.

'Drink that, Captain. It's the best whiskey. It will do you good. How are you feeling?'

'Not good,' Moran replied. He did not touch the whiskey. 'That blow has put paid to my work for the evening. It's the second time I've taken a blow on the head since I arrived, and if I'm not careful I might get some sense knocked into me.'

'I've tried that treatment on Wilbur, but it doesn't work.' Bowtell grinned. 'You haven't been introduced to him, Captain. This is Wilbur Giddings. He's not much to look at, and not any good at his job.'

'I said I was sorry,' Giddings snarled in a low voice, his eyes glinting momentarily as he regarded Moran through half-closed lids.

'We have to be getting back to town,' said Bowtell abruptly. 'Fetch the horses, Wilbur.' The deputy left immediately. 'I guess I'll see you around town some time,' continued Bowtell, looking at Moran. 'I guess you'll keep Shorten here behind bars until he's been charged, huh, Captain?'

'That's the way it will go,' Moran told him. He got to his feet and walked unsteadily to the door.

No one spoke as he left, and he stepped into the shadows beyond the doorway to stand with his shoulders pressed against the wall. He had no intention of calling off his night's duty, and was prepared to go to hell and back to gain proof of wrongdoing. He watched Bowtell leave the store and disappear among the shadows surrounding headquarters. A few moments later, two saddle horses passed him, one of them being ridden by Giddings. He watched

Giddings halt. Bowtell appeared, climbed into his saddle, and both lawmen rode to the gate and departed.

When the farrier sergeant emerged from the store and went his way, Moran entered and confronted Reinhardt. The sutler was seated at his desk, and he looked up at Moran with unchanging expression.

'Feeling better now, Captain?' he asked.

'I'd like an answer to a question that's bothering me,' Moran said.

'I've told you I will help in any way I can.'

'Why did you give the town marshal a wad of notes? I saw you pass them over just before the deputy struck me, and I heard what was said. What's your crooked game, Reinhardt?'

'That blow you took on the head must have been harder than Giddings thought,' Reinhardt replied. 'I gave Bowtell some papers needed at the bank, and he'll deliver them for me in the morning. No money changed hands.'

Moran slid his pistol out of its holster and covered Reinhardt. 'You're lying, and I'm arresting you on suspicion of wrongdoing. You'll be held while an investigation is carried out. If you have a gun on you then get rid of it quickly.'

Reinhardt reached into an inside pocket and produced a small calibre pistol, which he tossed to Moran, who instinctively grabbed at it. Reinhardt stepped forward a short pace and swung his clenched right hand. His bunched knuckles caught Moran on the chin and sent him staggering sideways, but he recovered quickly and threw a solid punch at the sutler's jaw.

Reinhardt fell instantly, but squirmed around and surged to his feet. Moran had lost his grip on his gun and Reinhardt made a dive for it. Moran kicked out and the solid toe of his boot slammed into Reinhardt's face. The sutler hit the floor with his chin, and Moran moved in quickly and retrieved his gun. Reinhardt looked up to stare into the unwavering muzzle. . . .

The guardhouse was silent, and a single lamp burned in the duty room. Moran followed Reinhardt into the office. Sergeant Comer was sitting at a desk, and got to his feet and saluted when he saw Moran.

'Sergeant, I've arrested Reinhardt on suspicion of being involved in nefarious activities with others at present unknown. He's to be held isolated behind bars until I've investigated him. Is that clear?'

'Yes, Captain.' Comer was surprised but picked up a bunch of keys from a corner of his desk and began to lead the way to the cells.

'Empty your pockets, Reinhardt,' Moran said. 'Check his belongings, Sergeant, and make a list of them. Report to the orderly officer and acquaint him with the charge.'

Moran waited until Reinhardt was locked in a cell and then took his leave. He hurried to the stable and saddled his horse. A charge had been made and he had to get the proof to make it stick. That proof was in the town marshal's pocket. Moran sent his horse from the fort and rode as fast as conditions permitted in order to reach town close behind Bowtell, and he caught up with Bowtell and Giddings as they reached the barn on the back lot behind the jail. He tethered his mount in an alley, and was waiting for Bowtell when the deputy town marshal hurried off to the saloon and Bowtell let himself into the law office.

Drawing his gun, Moran put a hand on the panel of the door and prevented Bowtell from closing it. Bowtell cursed and pulled the door wide, and astonishment showed on his face when he saw Moran with his pistol levelled.

'What the hell are you doing here, Captain?' Bowtell demanded. 'I thought you'd be tucked up in your bed by now, after that whack Giddings gave you.'

'I've got some questions to ask you, Bowtell.' Moran followed the town marshal into the office and closed the door with his heel. Bowtell started his hand to his gun but Moran beat him to the weapon and snatched it out of its holster. 'Empty your pockets on the table and then we'll get down to business.'

Bowtell gazed at him, his face expressionless. Moran did not move. His gaze was intent. Bowtell shrugged his heavy shoulders and emptied his pockets, but kept his hand away from the inside jacket pocket where he had placed the wad of paper money Reinhardt had given him.

'What the hell is this?' Bowtell demanded. 'I ain't in the mood for games. I've had a long day and I need to hit the sack.'

111

'You've got a wad of greenbacks in your inside pocket. I saw Reinhardt give it to you,' Moran said. 'I need them as evidence, and I want a sworn statement from you saying how those notes came into your possession, and don't give me any lies. I heard what Reinhardt said to you when he handed over the money. Reinhardt is behind bars at the fort, so it will be in your interests to come clean about what's going on.'

Bowtell looked at him for some moments, his body rigid with tension. Moran could almost see what was passing through his mind. Then Bowtell shrugged and relaxed. He grimaced, sat down at his desk, and produced the money Reinhardt had given him. He threw it on the desk and looked defiantly at Moran.

'It looks like you got me to rights,' he admitted. 'So you heard what was said in Reinhardt's office, huh? That fool Giddings never did anything right, he should have got to you before you could listen in. OK, so I got some dough from Reinhardt, but I ain't telling you why. That's my business. So what happens now? Are you gonna lock me in my own jail?'

'I'll take you back to the fort and put you in the guardhouse,' Moran decided. 'That way I'll be sure of finding you in the morning.'

'There's a lot been happening around here that you won't even begin to straighten out, and it might pay you to do a deal with me. I'll disappear over the nearest hill and you'll be able to clean up with no trouble at all. How does that grab you?'

'No deal.' Moran shook his head. 'I'm making

headway with my investigation so I don't need any help from you.' He put the money into his pocket and motioned with his gun. 'Let's go,' he added. 'You're not the only one who needs some sleep, and I've got a busy day tomorrow.'

Bowtell was silent on the ride to the fort. Moran remained fully alert; half-expecting his prisoner to make an attempt to escape, but Bowtell remained motionless in his saddle, and stepped down from his mount when they arrived at the door of the guard-house. Sergeant Comer was at his desk, and got to his feet when he noted that Moran was holding a drawn gun.

'What's going on, Captain?' Comer saluted and remained at attention.

'I've arrested the town marshal and I want him held in close arrest while an investigation is made into his activities. Have you got a separate cell? He's not to be permitted to talk to anyone.'

'I can take care of that, sir,' Comer said.

Moran stood with his gun in his hand while Bowtell was searched, had all belongings removed, and was taken to a cell. Comer locked the cell door and faced Moran.

'Are there any special orders for the prisoner, sir?'

'Only that no one is allowed to talk to him.' Moran turned to leave. He paused in the doorway and looked back at the police sergeant. 'I'll be back in the morning. Has the sutler said anything since he's been in here?'

'He's not in here, Captain. Major Harmon

returned from town a short while ago, and came in when he heard Mr Reinhardt had been arrested. The Major said he would be responsible for the sutler, and I released him from custody. I know what you said, sir, but the Major gave me orders.'

'You did what?' Moran bellowed.

'There was nothing else I could do, sir. I had to obey the Major.'

'I want to see the town marshal in his cell in the morning,' Moran rapped. 'If by any chance the Major wants Bowtell released then refer him to me.'

'I'll do that, sir.'

Moran departed, went across to the officers' quarters, and tapped on Harmon's door. The Major jerked it open, and his expression hardened when he saw Moran.

'You want to see me about releasing Mr Reinhardt from close custody, eh?' Harmon said. 'I can assure you that he will be here when you want to talk to him.'

'That's not the point, Major. I arrested Reinhardt to prevent him contacting others who share his guilt. I've just returned from Cactusville with the town marshal under arrest, and I planned to question both men separately and get down in writing just what they've been doing around here. You had no right to turn Reinhardt loose, and I view your action as bad judgement.'

Harmon's expression hardened and his mouth pulled into a thin, uncompromising line. 'I don't want to pull rank on you, Captain,' he snapped, 'but

I am the commanding officer of this fort, and while you are here, you are under my command.'

'You are labouring under a misapprehension, Major. While I am in this fort and working on an investigation, I exceed all ranks and you cannot interfere.' Moran reached into his pocket, produced his papers, and selected a small card, which he thrust under Harmon's nose. 'Read that, Major, and note the signature. It is signed by General Whittaker, the commanding general of this military area, and states that I am to receive full co-operation, without let or hindrance, from everyone I approach, regardless of rank.'

'You didn't show this to me when you arrived,' Harmon blustered.

'Well now you've seen it, sir. I want Reinhardt back in the guardhouse immediately, and no interference in future. I hope I make myself clear, Major.'

'I'll send Sergeant Comer and two men to pick up Reinhardt and place him back behind bars, Captain,' Harmon said stiffly.

'I'll pick up Reinhardt myself.' Moran turned, departed, and went to the sutler's store.

He wondered why Harmon had interfered. Was the commanding officer involved in the trouble? Moran intended finding out, and it would be a bad day for anyone who disobeyed orders in the future.

He entered the store and discovered that Reinhardt was not there. A big man was seated at the sutler's desk, engaged in checking a couple of thick ledgers. He looked up at Moran when he was disturbed in his task, his dark eyes unfriendly, his fleshy face set in a harsh expression.

'What do you want, Captain?' he growled.

'Reinhardt! Where is he?'

'As far as I know he went into town, and left me with a pile of work to do.'

'Who are you and what is your job here?'

'I'm Gus Vernon, Reinhardt's manager.'

'Then you're just the man I need to talk to. You must know just about everything that goes on around here. What's the connection between Reinhardt and Bowtell, the town marshal?'

'Connection? I don't know what you mean, Captain.'

'I suspect you do, judging by your expression. There's a criminal connection between them and I am carrying out an investigation. If you have any knowledge at all about what's going on, you'd be well advised to tell me about it.'

Vernon shrugged. 'I'm still in the dark, Captain. You'll have to spell it out to me. I'm not aware of any-thing crooked going on. Mr Reinhardt is strictly honest. That's how he comes across to me. He does a good job here, and doesn't get much in the way of thanks for it.'

'I'll see that he gets justice,' said Moran sharply. 'Shut the store and come with me. I'll put you behind bars until morning. I'm sure you'll know the answers to most of the questions I'll ask.'

Vernon closed his ledgers with great deliberation and got up off his chair, his expression showing his feelings. Moran could see he would have trouble, and edged his hand closer to his holstered gun. Vernon came forward, his hands in plain view. As he passed Moran to the door, his right elbow lifted quickly and he reached for a gun under his coat. Moran saw a weapon appear in Vernon's fist and swung towards him.

Moran drew his pistol and presented the muzzle at Vernon, who quickly realized that he had lost the initiative and was in deep trouble. He released his grip on his gun before Moran could complete his move and was in the process of raising his hands when Moran struck him with the muzzle of his gun.

Vernon fell to the floor and made no attempt to move. Moran covered him. Vernon was breathing heavily, looking up at him and shaking his head.

'I'm not involved in anything, Captain,' he said quickly.

'So why did you resist?'

'Panic, I expect. I won't give you any more trouble.'

'You could have been killed.' Moran picked up Vernon's discarded weapon, a two-shot pocket gun, and dropped it into his pocket. 'Get up and head for the guardhouse,' he said. 'I guess you know where it is. And you'd better do a lot of thinking about your situation before I get around to questioning you in the morning.'

They went to the guardhouse, and Moran stood watching while Vernon was taken into custody. When the cell door was closed and locked, Moran peered at Vernon.

'Where will I find Reinhardt when I get to town?' he asked.

'You won't find him in town. He'll be at his cattle ranch four miles to the west of Cactusville. You'd do well to wait until daylight before thinking of arresting him. He's got a real salty crew out there, and they shoot first and ask questions afterwards, especially at night. It would be better to ask at the saloon for Bill Nielsen. Tell him I sent you, and he'll take you out to Reinhardt's place.'

'Why are you suddenly so helpful?' Moran demanded.

'I don't see any other way out of this fix,' Vernon replied.

Moran fetched his horse and set out for Cactusville. He rode through the black night, following the light-coloured trail that stretched out endlessly through the shadows. He was wary, regarding each shadow on the trail as if it were someone waiting to ambush him. When he reached town, he dismounted at the hitch rail in front of the saloon, wrapped his reins around the rail and went into the noisy building. The evening was now well advanced and the saloon was crowded. At the far end the pianist was playing a melody. Moran looked around for Ruth, and was disappointed not to see her. He went to the bar and called the bartender, who looked as if he was being run off his feet. When Moran asked for Nielsen, the 'tender shook his head.

'He ain't here right now. Reinhardt came in a short while ago and sent Nielson out on a job.

Nielsen said he wouldn't be back tonight; said he'd got another job to do later that wouldn't wait.'

'How do I get to Reinhardt's cattle spread from here?' Monroe asked.

The 'tender glanced around. 'That cowboy in the corner in the green shirt is Frank Donovan. I'll have a word with him and he'll likely agree to show you the way.'

Moran waited. The 'tender went across to the corner table and spoke to the man in the green shirt, who looked across at Moran and nodded. The 'tender returned.

'Donovan will be leaving in half an hour and he'll show you the way to Reinhardt's place,' the 'tender said.

Moran sat at a table with a glass of beer until the cowboy threw in his hand and got up from his seat. He came to Moran – a big man with a cheerful face and laughing blue eyes. He was dressed in range clothes, and his voice was affable when he spoke.

'You look like you've got some bad news for the boss,' Donovan said. 'He ain't in trouble, is he?'

'No, as a matter of fact, he isn't,' Moran replied. 'Why do you ask?'

'He always talks like that. Ask him how his business is going and he'll usually say he's expecting trouble.'

They left the saloon and Donovan fetched his horse from the livery barn. Moran went with him, leading his own horse, and when Donovan mounted a grey, they set off along a trail heading east. The moon was in the eastern half of the sky and cast long silver fingers of cold brilliance into the dark shadows on the range. Moran remained silent for most of the trip while Donovan talked about local conditions.

Reinhardt's range lay stark under the starlight. They clattered into the yard and Donovan reined in. Spots of yellow lamplight showed at lower windows in the shapeless pile of the ranch house, and brighter lights gleamed in several windows in a long, low building across the yard.

'That's the house over there,' said Donovan, pointing to the right. 'Ride straight over and knock at the door. There's a guard around somewhere who will have seen you come in with me. I'm for the bunkhouse – time to hit the sack.'

'Thanks for showing me the way,' Moran said, and Donovan moved off.

Moran rode across the yard and stepped down from his saddle. He wrapped his reins around a hitch rail and looked around, his right hand close to the butt of his holstered gun. As he stepped on to the porch and knocked on the ranch house door, a voice spoke from the heavy shadows along the porch, its owner invisible in the darkness between two windows.

'You're in uniform; so what's your business with Mr Reinhardt?'

'That's not for you to know,' Moran replied. 'Is Reinhardt here?'

'What do you want, Moran?' The house door opened at that moment and Reinhardt was silhouetted in the doorway.

'We have some unfinished business to discuss.' Moran moved towards Reinhardt, who stepped back into the house. 'No need to wait until tomorrow. There's no time like the present.'

'Come in then. Hey, Walker, be ready for trouble.'

'What kind of trouble?' the guard asked.

'If you don't know the answer then you're fired,' Reinhardt rasped.

Moran entered the house and closed the door. Reinhardt was in a dressing gown. He was smiling, which bothered Moran, for with the trouble facing him, Reinhardt should have been greatly worried.

'I had plans for interrogating you in the fort,' Moran said.

'You didn't expect me to remain behind bars, did you, when the Major turned me loose?' Reinhardt laughed. 'You don't have a chance, Moran. The cards are stacked against you.'

'I'm looking at the situation from a different aspect,' Moran said. 'My sums add up differently to yours. I can see the outline of the crookedness based on the fort – you, Major Harmon, and Bowtell are running it. All I have to do is secure the details, like where does Clark fit into the action. I'm beginning to think that he is not guilty of murder, as he says.'

'You've spoken to Clark?' Reinhardt's manner changed and his eyes expressed shock.

Moran observed the sutler for several moments, and then laughed harshly. 'I wouldn't want to be in your boots when the facts of what's been going on start coming out. If you want any chance of getting out of this with the minimum of trouble then you'd better start co-operating with me. In these crime combines, the top men usually get away with it because they've covered their tracks, but there are always some who carry the can, and they end up with the book being thrown at them. You look like being one of the losers who will be left holding the bag, and there are at least two murders to be hung around someone's neck.'

'I don't know anything about crime. I have nothing to hide. Check my books and ask around town. I'm clean, Captain, and always have been. If there is anything bad going on around here then you can take it from me that I am not involved.'

'When I overheard you talking at the fort with Marshal Bowtell, you handed a wad of greenbacks to him and said you were halting all activities until I had finished my investigation. Bowtell offered to kill me but you didn't want that. So you are lying through your teeth when you say your slate is clean. When I arrested Bowtell, he saw instantly that there was no way out for him and he admitted being a part of the trouble, but he would not talk about why you gave him that dough so I'm asking you. Stop wasting my time, and if you take my advice, you'll tell the truth and hope there's a loophole somewhere through which you can escape. It's your only chance, and if you miss it, you'll stand accused with the rest of the guilty men I'm going to round up.'

The door opened at that moment and two men entered. One was Donovan, who had brought Moran to the ranch, and the other was the guard on duty on the porch. Donovan was holding a pistol in his hand, the muzzle aimed unerringly at Moran. The guard moved to one side to cover Moran from another angle.

'I'm sorry to interrupt you, boss,' Donovan said, 'but I got to thinking about bringing this man into the ranch. Did I do right?'

'You did wrong,' Reinhardt said, grinning. 'But you're doing the right thing now so I forgive you. Disarm the Captain and hogtie him. He knows too much. I want you and Walker to take him out on the range and kill him. He's bad trouble, so don't make any mistakes. Kill him and bury him deep.'

NINE

Moran was taken completely by surprise, and with two guns covering him from different angles, he was unable to attempt to turn the tables on these alert-eyed men. He stood motionless while Donovan came forward to disarm him, and the cowboy grinned as he lifted Moran's pistol from its holster.

'Nothing personal,' he said. 'Just don't try anything. I'm wise to all the tricks.'

'While you're at it, Donovan, there's a female up in the front bedroom. She's the singer from the big saloon in town. She's been asking a lot of questions about the fort. Someone said she is a sister of that lieutenant who was shot dead in the fort from Spyglass Hill.'

'Lieutenant Sandwell,' Donovan said. 'What do you want me to do with her?'

'Kill two birds with one stone. Take her along with Moran and bury them both.'

Moran was shocked by the news, and remained motionless and silent with Walker's rifle covering him. Reinhardt led Donovan up to the bedrooms. Moran recognized Ruth's voice as she was brought protesting down the stairs, and his thoughts swirled with conjecture as he wondered how she had managed to get herself caught up in this dangerous situation.

Ruth was bustled into the bottom room, protesting and struggling in Donovan's strong grip and, when she saw Moran standing motionless under guard, she became still and fell silent, gazing at him in astonishment.

'What are you doing here, Captain?' she demanded. 'I was hoping you were getting to grips with these bad men and would come and save me from them, but it looks like you're in the same plight as me.'

'I am temporarily at a disadvantage,' Moran said. 'But there's nothing to worry about.'

'That's putting it mildly.' Reinhardt grinned. 'I'm sorry to disappoint you, Miss Sandwell, but Captain Moran has understated the situation. He's on his way to a lonely grave on the range and you're going with him. You two can share a grave, so it won't be so lonely.' He looked at Donovan. 'You know what to do so don't slip up. Do this right and come back here afterwards.'

'Sure, boss.' Donovan pushed Moran in the back. 'Get moving. I need to get some sleep before sun up.'

They left the ranch house. Donovan left Moran and Ruth on the porch under the menace of Walker's rifle and went to fetch horses for himself and the girl. Moran glanced into Ruth's face as she gazed into the lamplight issuing from a window. He had two small guns in his pockets, but he wanted to get away from the ranch before attempting an escape. He had no idea how many men Reinhardt employed at the ranch, and he needed the odds to be as short as possible.

Donovan returned, riding his horse and leading another. He dismounted at the porch and drew his pistol as he confronted Moran.

'Get your hands up,' he grated. 'I want to search you, and then I'll tie you to your saddle. Give me any trouble and you'll be dead before you reach your last resting place.'

Moran raised his hands, aware that he had made a bad mistake in not attempting to overpower these men while he had a chance. He clenched his teeth as Donovan took his pistols. His hands were tied and Donovan roped him in his saddle before handling Ruth in the same manner.

They left the ranch. Donovan led the way, followed by Moran and Ruth, and Walker brought up the rear. They travelled at a lope through the shadows, and when they reached the open range, they slowed to a trot. Moran looked around.

'I don't think you're so stupid you'll obey Reinhardt's orders,' Moran said. 'Turn me loose now, Donovan, and save yourself a heap of trouble.'

'No chance,' Donovan replied. 'The boss gives orders and we obey. That's the way it works around here.'

'So tell me what's been going on. There's been trouble at the fort, and I've already worked out that Reinhardt is behind it, along with Bowtell.'

'You know too much,' Donovan said. 'That's why you're going to sleep out on the prairie. If you know any prayers you'd better start saying them. You ain't got much longer. There's a nice little spot in a gully just ahead. Several men are buried out here, so you'll have some company. Now button your lip.'

Moran made vain efforts to loosen the rope around his wrists before he gave up trying. Ruth spoke to Donovan, asking about her brother – why he had been killed, and who murdered him.

'Why ask me?' Donovan demanded. 'I don't know anything about what's been going on at the fort. You should have asked the boss while we were at the ranch. Reinhardt has all the answers. You keep quiet now and we'll put you away nice and easy.'

Moran had experienced some bad moments in his time, but nothing like this. He could see no way out. He did not expect Donovan to untie him, and he began to wonder if this was the end of his trail. He glanced at Ruth, riding at his side, her face pale in the starlight, taut and set with fear about what was going to happen to her. He felt a pang of pity for her, and something else that came from deep within him. He attacked his bonds again, with no success.

'I wish I knew what happened to my brother,' Ruth said suddenly. 'Why don't you tell me?' she asked Donovan. 'You're in this trouble up to your neck so you must be aware of what's been happening.'

'Just shut your mouth,' Donovan replied. 'Your brother was a spy at the fort. He was poking around and asking questions about everyone. Just like you were doing in town. So he was killed to shut his mouth.'

'Who killed him?' Ruth's voice quivered.

'That's the big question for you, huh?' Donovan laughed. 'And you'll never know the answer. What kind of an idiot do you take me for? In this business you keep your mouth shut or wind up dead—'

'We're at the gully,' Walker interrupted. 'It's just to the right. Let's get this over with quickly.'

'Are you losing your nerve?' Donovan asked, and laughed brutally.

'I'm not keen on killing a woman,' Walker replied. 'She ain't done anything. It was her brother who was spying on us.'

'What do you think she's been doing while she's been in town?'

'Well, I don't like it.' Walker's tone turned sullen.

'Do you want to join them in the gully?' Donovan demanded.

'The hell I do! And I ain't gonna stand by and watch a woman get slaughtered. You're a cold-blooded killer, Donovan. It don't bother you none, but it bothers me.'

They were reining in on the lip of a gully at the foot of a long slope. Donovan stepped down from his saddle and turned to untie Moran. Walker dismounted and approached Ruth.

'Get back and watch Moran closely,' Donovan

snarled at him. 'He's the dangerous one, so don't give him even half a chance.'

Walker grumbled, stepped back a couple of paces and covered Moran with his pistol. Donovan untied Moran and pushed him into the gully. Moran fell on his face and rolled on to his back. He looked up. Donovan was peering down at him, his pistol lined up on his chest.

'This is it,' Donovan grated.

A shot crashed. Moran clenched his teeth, tensed for the impact of a slug. But there was no flash from Donovan's gun, and Donovan cried out as a bullet struck him in the back. He fell forward and toppled into the gully, his gun spilling from his hand. Moran rolled aside, and then threw himself on top of Donovan, his hands scrabbling in the deeply shadowed gully to locate Donovan's dropped gun.

Moran's fingers closed on the pistol and he thrust himself up on to his knees. The echoes of the shot were fading away into the distance, but his attention was centred on Walker, standing motionless, gun down at his side.

'Who is out there?' Moran called.

'There's no one out there,' said Walker. 'I shot Donovan. I've had enough of his bullying ways, the killing and the stealing. And he was intent on murdering an innocent woman! It goes to show how low this bunch has sunk.'

'You're free to ride out of here,' Moran said.

Walker holstered his gun. Moran heaved a sigh of relief as he turned and freed Ruth, who fell against him as the rope dropped from her. He caught her and supported her, his gaze on Walker's face.

'You'd better ride a long way from here, Walker,' Moran said. 'Reinhardt is running a bad bunch.'

'I'll be long gone by sun up,' Walker replied. He turned away, walked to his horse and swung into the saddle. 'Good luck to you, Moran. I hope you'll come out on top.'

'You've given me a fighting chance,' Moran replied.

Walker rode off into the night. Ruth began to stir in Moran's arms, and he held her gently until she recovered her senses. She looked around quickly, and gasped when she realized they were alone.

'It's OK,' he said. 'Walker shot Donovan, and he's gone now. We're on our own. I'd better take you to the fort. You'll be safe with the military. But I'd like to sneak back into Reinhardt's yard and surprise him. With him behind bars, most of my problems will be over.'

'Go for him before taking me back to the fort,' Ruth said eagerly. 'He's been giving the orders around here so he'll know who killed my brother.'

Moran shook his head. 'I'm taking you out of danger and I'll ensure that nothing else bad happens to you,' he replied.

Ruth shook her head. 'Just let me do this thing,' she urged. 'I can't live the rest of my life on a knife-edge. I need to do what I have to do.'

'All right, I'll take you along. But you'll have to stay back out of danger while I arrest Reinhardt.'

'I promise,' she said fervently.

They mounted their horses and rode back to Reinhardt's ranch. It was around midnight when they sighted the spread, which was in complete darkness. Moran halted fifty yards out from the yard and looked around.

'You'll have to take cover somewhere around here,' he mused. 'And stay put until I come for you. Ignore anything that happens, and if it looks like I've failed then you'd better hightail it to the fort and talk to Sergeant-Major Craven; on no account try to approach Reinhardt or Major Harmon.'

'I'll do like you say,' Ruth said. 'Please be careful.'

'Careful is my middle name,' he responded.

She dismounted and led her horse into cover. 'I've got a derringer in my pocket,' she said, and I'll use it if I have to.' She sank down out of sight in the long grass.

'I shouldn't be too long,' he told her, and rode on to the ranch.

He left his horse outside the yard and walked towards the house, keeping to the shadows. Silence enveloped him. The breeze was cool in his face. He expected to see a guard but there was no sign of life. He dropped to one knee, gun in hand, and checked the shadows. He saw nothing suspicious, and was about to move on when he caught the smell of cigarette smoke on the breeze. It was gone in a flash but he tensed and waited. Several moments later, a shadow appeared around a corner of the house and disappeared into the blackness of the porch. He heard the sound of a loose board creak under the weight of a boot.

The guard passed along the porch and appeared on the other side of the house. He paused for a few moments, and then crossed to the bunk house. A door rattled, and lamplight filled a window with yellow glare. Moran closed in and peered into the bunk house. A man was in the act of propping a rifle in a corner beside a bunk, and he drew the makings of a cigarette from his breast pocket. Moran entered the bunk house, gun in hand, as the man struck a match.

Moran was surprised when he noticed there was no one else in the bunk house. The guard was turning to face him, and when he saw that Moran was a stranger, he dropped a hand to the butt of his holstered pistol.

'Forget your gun,' Moran snapped. 'Remove it from your holster and throw it in a corner.' He waited until the guard had complied. 'Where's the crew?' he continued. 'The place is empty.'

'They rode out with the boss,' the man replied. 'Something came up that needed Reinhardt and some of the boys to handle it.'

'Where have they gone?'

'No one tells me anything around here.' The guard shook his head. 'They upped and left, and that's all I can tell you.'

'Which way did they ride when they pulled out?'

'I didn't see them go. Who are you, Captain? I guess you're one of Reinhardt's friends, huh?'

'We're very close.' Moran smiled, and turned to leave. He moved to one side of the door and paused, but there was no reaction from the man inside.

Moran went back to where he had left Ruth. She did not appear until he called her name, and then materialized from deep shadow, holding a small pocket gun ready for action. Moran was impressed by her determination.

'What happened?' she demanded. 'I didn't hear any shooting.'

'Reinhardt has pulled out with his crew. I've got no idea where they went, but I expect it means trouble for someone on the range.'

'What can we do now?'

'We are going to do nothing.' Moran shook his head. 'But I know what you're going to do. I'll take you to the fort and ensure that you'll be safe. Then I'll get on with my job.'

He fetched her horse and helped her to mount. They rode through the darkness to the fort, and discovered great activity taking place inside. The garrison was mounted and formed up on the square. Major Harmon was facing his command, and his officers were also on parade. Moran reined in on the edge of the square with Ruth beside him, and they watched the troopers wheel their mounts and begin to ride out of the gate. Harmon saw Moran but made no move to confront him. The whole garrison departed, and Ruth looked up at Moran.

'Where are they going?' she asked.

'Your guess is as good as mine,' he replied. 'I'll

find someone to talk to. There'll be a guard around, and he should know what's going on.'

A figure appeared on the veranda in front of the administration block, silhouetted against lamp light, and Moran recognized Sergeant-Major Craven. He rode across the parade ground with Ruth close to his side. Craven saluted when he spotted Moran.

'What's going on, Sergeant-Major?' Moran demanded.

'Major Harmon has taken everyone out on a night patrol,' Craven replied. 'There's only a small guard left here. It's to do with discipline, sir, or the lack of it. By the time they ride back here tomorrow, there'll be a different attitude among the men.'

Moran grimaced; the running of the fort had nothing to do with him.

'I've got Miss Sandwell here. She fell into the wrong hands earlier, and I've brought her into the fort for her safety. I want you to take care of her until tomorrow morning. I expect to settle the trouble here before too long. Are my prisoners still behind bars?'

'Yes, Captain.'

'I'll go to the guardhouse and get statements. I have enough evidence to pin some of the guilt where it belongs, and when the truth starts appearing, it won't be long before the whole crooked business erupts.'

'Can't I stay with you, Captain?' Ruth appealed to him.

'It will be better for you to stay under the Sergeant-Major's wing,' Moran told her. 'Try and get some sleep. You've had a bad experience, and tomorrow I shall need a full statement from you about what happened tonight. You'll figure prominently in my investigation.'

Ruth permitted Craven to lead her away and Moran went to the guardhouse. Sergeant Comer admitted him.

'Is everything OK, Sergeant?' Moran asked.

'All quiet, sir,' Comer replied. 'The sutler's manager, Vernon, has been complaining about being held behind bars. He wants to see Reinhardt as soon as possible.'

'So do I!' Moran smiled. 'Give me your keys, Sergeant. I want to talk to the men I arrested.'

Comer handed over his keys and Moran went into the cells. He looked through the barred door of the nearest cell and saw Bowtell stretched out on the bunk, apparently asleep, eyes closed, his breathing regular. Moran remained silent and motionless, and Bowtell's eyelids began to flicker as moments passed. Finally Bowtell's eyes opened and he stared at Moran.

'What the hell do you want?' he demanded.

'A written statement from you, duly signed.'

'Nothing doing. I'm not putting anything down on paper, and I've said all I'm gonna say. I told you I'd do a deal, but you're not interested, so go ahead and do your job the hard way.'

'I've got all the time in the world,' Moran said, 'and I'll keep you behind bars until you do talk.'

'I want to see a lawyer,' said Bowtell obstinately.

135

Moran looked into the next cell and saw Gus Vernon pacing the length of his cell. Vernon halted, glared at Moran when he became aware of his presence, and came to the door of the cell and gripped the bars.

'How long are you gonna keep me penned in here?' Vernon demanded. 'I've done nothing wrong, and I want to see the lawyer. I'm not in the Army so you can't hold me. I demand to be set free. Where's Reinhardt? Why isn't he in here instead of me? He's been fiddling the books, but I'm innocent.'

'All in good time,' Moran told him. 'Make a statement about what's been going on in the fort involving Reinhardt and maybe you'll get out of here before the snow flies.'

Moran went to the next cell, his eyes narrowing when he saw Shorten sitting on a bunk, his expression ferocious, a cigarette held in his left hand.

'I haven't forgotten about you, Shorten,' Moran said. 'Have you got anything to say about your business with Major Harmon? I know there was a crooked deal going on between you two.'

Shorten scowled and averted his face, drawing hard on his cigarette.

'Why did you kill Sergeant Bessemer?' asked Moran in a brutal tone.

Shorten looked into Moran's eyes and grinned but said nothing.

Sergeant Comer came into the cell block. 'Can I have the keys, sir? My relief is outside.'

Moran handed over the keys and the sergeant

departed. He heard the main entrance being unlocked and the door was opened. Then there was the sound of a blow and Sergeant Comer cried out. A body fell to the floor. Moran ran into the front office, drawing his gun. He saw Sergeant Comer lying on the floor, and six men were crowding into the office, all holding pistols. Reinhardt was leading them, and the sutler uttered a yell and lifted his gun to aim at Moran, who fired swiftly. Reinhardt pitched to the floor. Moran stepped back into the cell block as the men with Reinhardt turned to came into action, and the silence was ripped apart by hammering guns. . . .

TEN

A fusillade of shots bracketed the doorway to the cells. Splinters flew from the woodwork. Moran controlled his surprise. He slammed the door, slid home a thick iron bolt, and then stepped back from the door. Bowtell came to the bars of his cell door, grinning.

'I offered you a deal,' he said. 'Now it's too late.'

'Sit down and keep your mouth shut,' Moran snapped. He backed out of the line of fire; slugs were boring through the thick door and slamming into the cells. Voices were shouting in the outer office, and Moran wondered what had happened to Reinhardt.

He glanced along the passage leading to a back door, ran to it, and was shocked to find it was not locked, and the iron bolt was out of its socket. The door opened to his touch and he peered outside. The shadows were dense but a pistol was fired from the right and a red streak of muzzle flame cut through the night. A bullet slammed into the door close by Moran's head. He fired instantly, aiming for the flash, and then slipped out of the doorway and ran to his left. Another gun fired at him and he heard the bullet crackle into woodwork close by. He fired in reply and the gun fell silent. He kept moving, wanting to get around the guardhouse to the main entrance.

He heard voices shouting nearby, and guessed that the detail left behind to guard the fort was waking up to the fact that the fort was being attacked. He slid around the rear corner of the guardhouse and walked into a man coming from the opposite direction. Moran twisted sideways and missed the full force of the advancing body. The man yelled in surprise. Moran swung his pistol and slammed the muzzle against the man's head. He followed him down to the ground and struck a second blow. The man relaxed instantly. Moran searched him for weapons.

The man was not in uniform, and Moran guessed he was one of Reinhardt's men. He got to his feet and ran alongside the guardhouse to the front corner and stepped around it with his pistol raised. A man was standing in the open doorway of the guardhouse, keeping watch on the parade ground. He spotted Moran's movement and lifted his pistol. Moran shot him and ran forward. He kicked the man's gun away from the motionless body and kept moving, stepping across the threshold into the guardhouse.

Moran saw Reinhardt lying on the floor inside.

Blood was dribbling from the sutler's chest. He was semi-conscious, his face pale, eyes half-closed. Near him was the inert body of Sergeant Comer, who had a trickle of blood at his mouth and a large bruise on his forehead. A man was standing by the desk just inside the entrance, and he spun around at the sound of Moran's feet, reaching for his holstered gun. Moran struck the man's gun wrist as he drew a weapon, and then hit him squarely in the face with his gun barrel.

As the man went down, Moran ran to the door to the cells. He could hear voices coming from inside the cells, and stepped into the doorway just as Bowtell appeared. The town marshal was holding a pocket pistol, and he cursed at the sight of Moran and tried to throw himself backwards out of the doorway, at the same time swinging his gun to cover Moran.

Moran fired at the exact instant that Bowtell's pistol blasted. Moran's shot struck Bowtell in the chest. The crooked town marshal fell backwards, his boots clattering on the stone floor. Two men were unlocking other cell doors, but the shooting distracted them and they swung quickly to confront Moran. Guns flamed and hammered. Gun smoke drifted.

Moran was fast and deadly. His first shot took one of the men through the neck, and he fell sideways against his companion, hindering his draw. The second man's gun flamed and the bullet went up through the roof. Moran clamped his teeth together and squeezed his trigger as his foresight lined up on its target. When he fired, the man jerked sideways and then flattened out on the floor, blood spilling from his chest.

Moran pushed himself to his feet. The cells were filled with gun thunder and powder smoke. Gus Vernon, in the act of emerging from his cell when the shooting started, ducked back and dived to the floor. He sat up and looked around as silence returned, his face ashen, his forehead beaded with sweat. He saw Moran standing in the doorway of the cell, gun covering him, and jumped to his feet and came to Moran.

'I want to make a statement,' he gabbled. 'I'm not involved in any of this and yet I'm being shot at.'

'You said you wouldn't make a statement,' Moran reminded him.

'That was before all this shooting started. I want out, so I'll tell you what I know.'

'What do you know?' Moran countered.

'For a start I can tell you what happened to Trooper Clark.'

'I'm listening.'

'Everyone knew why Lieutenant Sandwell was here at the fort. He had been sent in under cover to check on crookedness, and Clark became friendly with him. Sandwell began to find out things and Reinhardt said Clark was giving Sandwell information. Clark was never one of Reinhardt's crew. So he had to be silenced, and was set up. They allowed him to escape, someone shot the guard Clark was charged with murdering, but they could not catch Clark afterwards.'

'Will you put that in writing and sign it?' Moran demanded.

Vernon nodded emphatically. 'Yes, any time you want it so long as it gets me out of here.'

'Give me the names of other men involved in the business.'

Vernon hesitated, his expression changing. 'I'll tell you that Reinhardt gave Bowtell $500 to kill Lieutenant Sandwell.'

Moran backed off. He closed the door of Vernon's cell and gazed into his eyes.

'Sandwell was shot by a sniper on Spyglass Hill, wasn't he?'

'Bowtell borrowed a special rifle from the gun shop in town.' Vernon sighed heavily and turned to sit down on his bunk. He lowered his head to his hands in despair.

Moran turned when a voice called from the office, and he recognized Sergeant-Major Craven's voice. He peered out of the cell block. Craven was standing by the desk near the entrance, supporting Sergeant Comer, who was regaining his senses. Four tough troopers were standing in the doorway, armed and alert. Reinhardt was no longer in the office.

'Be with you in a moment, Sergeant-Major,' Moran called.

He went back into the cells, located the keys, and locked Vernon's cell door. He checked Bowtell. The crooked town marshal was dead.

Craven came into the cells. 'What happened here, Captain?'

'Reinhardt decided to free some of the prisoners but failed. I shot Reinhardt and he went down. I saw he'd gone when I came out to the office to talk to you.'

'Two riders were heading out of the gate when I came here to check on the shooting,' Craven said. 'That must have been Reinhardt pulling out.'

'He won't get far. Get this place cleaned up and remove the bodies. Is Miss Sandwell safe?'

'She's in the officers' quarters, and there's a guard at her door.'

'I'll get after Reinhardt again.' Moran departed.

He fetched his horse and rode to the gate. The sentry saluted.

'Two men rode out a few minutes ago,' Moran said. 'Did you recognize them?'

'It was Mr Reinhardt, the sutler, and a man I didn't know.'

'Did you see which direction they took?'

'They headed for town pretty damn quick.'

Moran touched spurs to his horse and departed in a hurry, riding for Cactusville, thinking over what Vernon had told him. He couldn't wait now to see Clark again, certain that the man had been telling the truth when he said he had not killed the sentry. He was satisfied that the facets of his investigation were falling nicely into place. The bad men were beginning to fall over themselves to talk.

The town was still, ready for the coming night, and

only the big saloon had lights burning and sound coming from it. Moran looked around for tethered horses but saw none.

He dismounted at a rail in front of the saloon and wrapped his reins around it, pausing to check his gun before entering the building.

Inside, poker was being played at a table, and several men stood around watching the game. Moran's eyes glinted when he looked at two men standing at the bar, for one of them was Clark. He went to Clark's side. Clark dropped a hand to his holstered gun when he realized someone was approaching him, but stayed his hand when he recognized Moran.

'Still looking for guilty men, Captain?' Clark asked.

'I've put some guilty men behind bars at the fort,' Moran told him. 'And I have word that you were set up by Reinhardt, that you're innocent of the charge of murder.'

'That's good news.' Clark smiled and relaxed. 'What happens now?'

'When I get the statement in writing and signed then you'll be off the hook.'

'You'd better tell the town marshal before he sets eyes on me,' Clark said.

'Forget about Bowtell. He's dead. I put him in the guardhouse earlier this evening and Reinhardt showed up with some men and tried to take over the guardhouse. I had to kill Bowtell.'

'It gets better and better,' Clark said. 'Bowtell was

in with Reinhardt.'

'I know that, too. We'd better get together soon and you can tell me what you know.'

'I've been finding out things,' Clark said. 'Major Harmon framed Colonel Davis, and the Colonel went sick. Harmon took over at the fort and began pushing for a bigger deal from Reinhardt.'

'That ties in with why the Major took the garrison out of the fort tonight,' Moran mused, 'to give Reinhardt the opportunity to attack the guardhouse and free the prisoners. Reinhardt had already caught me at his ranch and ordered a couple of men to kill me.'

'And they failed.' Clark looked at Moran with respect in his eyes. 'So what happens now?'

'I'll get statements where needed and ask questions until I get at the truth. I'd like to take you back to the fort with me and sort out your problems. If anything should happen to me before I can clear you then you could still be in trouble.'

'Does that mean me going back into the guardhouse?' asked Clark, his expression stiffening.

'No. I don't think I could take that risk while Major Harmon is on the loose with most of the garrison. I don't know how far this trouble has spread through the ranks. You'd better remain out of sight in town until Harmon returns and I can get the drop on him. Can you hide out around here?'

Clark smiled. 'I haven't been doing badly, have I?' he countered.

'You're right. I'll come back to town tomorrow

morning after Major Harmon has returned with the troopers. That will be the crunch-time. I need the Major behind bars to maintain control. Now I want to check with the doctor before I leave. Reinhardt was wounded when he escaped from the fort, and as he can't seek help from the Army doctor then he's probably come into town to see the local doctor. I'll see you tomorrow, Clark. Keep out of sight and trouble until then.'

Clark nodded. Moran turned to leave, and paused when he saw two soldiers pushing through the batwings to enter the saloon. Clark grasped Moran's arm and dragged him around the end of the bar and through a doorway that led into a store room.

'You're in trouble, Captain,' said Clark, his face tense. 'I do know some of the troopers who are in Reinhardt's pay, and those two coming through the batwings are part of the gang causing the trouble round here – Danson and Simmons. I'm wondering where the Major and the rest of the men are. If they are here to round you up then you're the one who has got to hide. Come on, I know how to get you out of here. Let's hope that Danson didn't spot you. He's got eyes like a hawk.'

Moran dropped a hand to his gun butt and eased the weapon in its holster. If Major Harmon was on the prowl then Moran wanted to face him, not hide from him. He looked around the store room – there didn't seem to be any means of escape from it. But Clark went to a door across the room and opened it to reveal a passage that led into the back area of the saloon. He motioned for Moran to follow him, moving quickly now, and Moran went without protest, aware that if he failed to take Harmon by surprise then he would probably lose the initiative and fail in his investigation.

Clark opened a second door at the end of the passage and they passed into the private area of the saloon, an office. A man was seated at a desk. He looked up quickly at their intrusion, and frowned at the sight of Moran in military uniform.

'What's going on, Clark?' the man demanded.

'It's OK, Frank. This is Captain Moran, a military policeman. He's at the fort to stamp out the trouble the Army is having. A couple of troopers just came in the front door, and the Captain doesn't want to be seen in here. We'll slip out your back door.'

'I hope you'll have good luck, Captain,' Frank Simpson said.

Clark went to a side door and opened it. Moran followed him, and a moment later, they were standing on the back lot in deep shadow.

'I'll see you to the doctor's house,' Clark said, and set off to the right and entered an alley that led to the main street.

They reached the street end of the alley and peered out to check the street. Moran grimaced when he saw six saddle horses outside the saloon, where his own mount was tethered.

'Let's keep to the shadows,' Clark said. 'Doc Arnott lives along here. There's a light in his office so he's probably got a patient in there. Let's take a look.'

Moran was relieved when they reached an alley beside the doctor's house without incident. They paused for a moment in the alley, and Moran was about to go on when he heard the sound of hoofs along the street. He placed a warning hand on Clark's arm and they waited. A moment later two soldiers rode by, each holding a carbine ready for action.

'They're loaded for bear,' Clark whispered. 'It looks like Major Harmon has put out the word on you, Captain.'

The soldiers went on towards the saloon. Clark slipped out to the doctor's front door, and opened it as Moran joined him. They entered, and a woman appeared in a doorway just along the passage that led from the front door to the rear entrance.

'Hello, I'm Mrs Arnott. I expect you want to see the doctor,' she said. 'He's in the office. Just knock on the door.'

Clark knocked on the door, opened it, and Moran pushed forward to see who was visiting the doctor. He jerked his gun out of his holster when he saw Reinhardt stretched out on a couch, stripped to the waist, a bullet wound in his right shoulder. Reinhardt's eyes were closed, and he was holding a pistol. He opened his eyes, and gasped when he recognized Moran. Clark leapt forward to grab at Reinhardt's gun, and Moran could see that he would be too late. He levelled his pistol at Reinhardt and fired a shot that reverberated through the house. Moran cursed the noise, which would alert the sol-

148

diers, but he was satisfied with his shot, for the bullet smashed into Reinhardt's gun and sent it crashing to the floor.

ELEVEN

Blood spurted from Reinhardt's hand and he yelled in agony. Doctor Arnott, who was in a small room at the rear of the office, came hurrying through. He halted on the threshold, shocked into immobility.

'I'm sorry for the disturbance, Doctor,' Moran said. 'I'm here to arrest Reinhardt on a criminal charge and he resisted. Can I take him out of here? I need him behind bars at the fort.'

'He shouldn't be moved for several days at least,' Arnott replied. 'What has he done wrong?'

'I don't know the full extent of the charges yet.' Moran shook his head. 'Is he able to travel? I'll transport him in a wagon, if that will satisfy you. But I must have him under lock and key.'

'I'll stay here with him until he's ready to leave,' Clark volunteered.

Moran nodded. 'That's a good idea. I need to get back to the fort. But first I must talk to one of the soldiers in town to find out what their orders are.'

'They look like they're on the prod,' Clark

warned. 'They're either under orders, or are part of Reinhardt's crooked set-up.'

'And I need to know where they stand,' Moran mused. 'I'll get a wagon round here for Reinhardt and an escort to the fort. Are you sure you can handle this until I get help?'

'I'll be OK if you notify someone in authority that I'm no longer wanted for desertion and murder.'

'I'll take care of it.' Moran smiled. 'Don't take any chances with Reinhardt.'

'Before you go,' Clark said, 'there are one or two things you should know. Lieutenant Sandwell's death – it was Bowtell who shot him. Harmon wanted him dead so Bowtell came into the fort early one morning and climbed up to the top of the water tank behind the horse lines. He shot Sandwell from up there, and everyone thought the bullet came from a sniper on Spyglass Hill.'

'Can you prove that?' Moran said.

'Not while Major Harmon is out of jail. Pin something on him and the rest of the trouble will collapse like a kite in a hurricane. There are a number of soldiers waiting for the day when someone like you will pull Harmon from his high saddle.'

'That's good to know.' Moran nodded. 'Take care on your way to the fort.'

Moran left the office and went back along the street to where a group of soldiers was standing with their mounts in front of the saloon. They were chatting loudly, but a silence descended quickly when Moran was seen.

'Who is in command here?' Moran said.

A Corporal stepped forward. 'I'm Corporal Eke, sir. Sergeant Tucker is inside the saloon. He got orders from Major Harmon to bring a detachment into town to hunt for Clark.'

'Do you know who I am, Corporal?' Moran said.

'Yes, sir. You're Captain Moran, in charge of the investigation going on at the fort.'

'I have news for you.' Moran raised his voice. 'I've almost finished my investigation, and one of the facts I've discovered is that Trooper Clark is innocent of all charges made against him. At the moment he is helping me with my investigation. He's at the doctor's house with Reinhardt, the fort sutler. Corporal, send two men to the stable and get a wagon. I want Reinhardt taken to the fort under guard and lodged in the guardhouse until I return there. Clark is acting under my orders, and he is to be treated as such. Is that clear?'

'Yes, sir, Captain.'

'Then inform your sergeant of the change of orders, in particular about Trooper Clark, and get things moving. I'm on my way back to the fort now, and I'm in a hurry.'

The Corporal shouted orders to the troopers, and hurried into the saloon as his men dispersed to obey him. Moran went to his horse and swung into the saddle. As he turned to ride out of town, a sergeant emerged from the saloon and called to him.

'Captain, I have orders from Major Harmon to arrest you on sight.'

Moran reined in and looked down at the sergeant, who was holding his pistol although it was not levelled at Moran. The soldiers paused and turned to see the outcome of the challenge, and Moran nodded.

'I'm giving you new orders, Sergeant. Trooper Clark is holding the sutler, Reinhardt, prisoner at the doctor's house. You and your men are to see that Clark and his prisoner arrive safely at the fort. Clark is no longer facing charges of murder and desertion. I have evidence that clears him. When you get to the fort, report to me.'

There was silence for several moments while the sergeant considered.

'What about Major Harmon's orders, Captain?'

'Always obey the last order, Sergeant. I shall be seeing the Major, and I'll bring him up to date with the situation.'

'Yes, sir.' The sergeant saluted.

Moran sighed with relief, sent his horse forward along the street, and rode out of town. He set off for the fort, hoping that all he had to do was talk to Major Harmon, arrest him, and he would have enough evidence to bring the case to a close. He travelled at a lope, following the dim line of the well-worn trail, fighting tiredness as he held himself in check. This case had not followed the usual routine of an investigation, of reading a summary of evidence, spotting the obvious pointers, and bringing pressure to bear upon the guilty until they broke down and confessed. . . .

The fort was unusually silent and still when Moran reined in at the front gate. A sentry emerged from the shadows at the entrance, holding a rifle, and he stiffened to attention and saluted when Moran halted before him.

'All is well, Captain,' the sentry reported.

Moran entered the fort and rode across the parade ground to where lights were shining in the administration area. Another sentry stepped out of the shadows and challenged him in a loud, clear tone and, as Moran gave his name, Sergeant Major Craven emerged from his office.

'Come into my office, Captain Moran,' Craven said. 'I've gathered statements from those men who were involved in the shooting in the guardhouse earlier.'

Moran followed the Sergeant-Major into the office, and pulled up short when he saw Major Harmon sitting at a desk, accompanied by Ruth Sandwell, who was looking very scared. Harmon had a pistol in his hand and it was cocked and pointing at Ruth.

'I've been waiting for you to get back here, Moran,' said Harmon harshly. 'Disarm yourself. I'm not taking any chances with you.'

'I've got some questions to ask you, Major,' Moran countered. 'Put down your gun, or better yet, give it to Sergeant-Major Craven.'

'No chance.' Harmon cocked the weapon and kept it aimed at Moran's chest.

'You took the garrison out of the fort earlier this

154

evening to give Reinhardt an opportunity to attack the guardhouse,' Moran continued. 'You've reached the end of your trail, Major.'

'Don't try to side-track me. Captain, I told you to disarm yourself, so do it now or I'll shoot you.'

'You don't have one chance of getting away with what you've done,' Moran replied. 'Before he died, Bowtell told me you were involved.' He glanced at Ruth Sandwell. 'Are you OK?' She grimaced, and he turned his attention to Sergeant-Major Craven. 'You were supposed to be taking care of Miss Sandwell,' he said.

Craven shrugged. 'Major Harmon returned to the fort unexpectedly and drew his gun on me. Now he is using Miss Sandwell as a hostage.'

'You'd better believe it, Moran.' Harmon tilted the muzzle, and fired a shot that reverberated in the small room. Gun smoke drifted with the fading echoes. 'I won't tell you again to divest yourself of your gun. My next shot will be through your head.'

Moran reached for his pistol with finger and thumb and lifted the weapon from its open-top holster. He threw it on the floor.

'So what happens now?' he demanded. 'Are you planning to kill all of us; everyone who knows what you've been doing?' He saw Harmon's change of expression and laughed mirthlessly. 'Half the men in the fort know what the trouble is around here. You've gone too far, Major, and now the chickens are coming home to roost. I've got Reinhardt coming back to the fort under armed guard, and he's given me enough of a statement to enable me to tie up the loose ends of this trouble. You'd better start thinking about your future. You've got to run from here as fast as you can, but I know from experience that you won't be able to hide from me. Evidence is reaching me fast and furious now your criminal scheme is running out of steam.'

'Who killed my brother, Major?' Ruth demanded. 'He came here to find out what was going on, and was shot dead for his trouble. Did you kill him? It sure was a nice touch to have him executed in front of his men.'

'I have no idea what happened to your brother.' Harmon's lips twisted as he spoke, and Moran smiled grimly.

'I received some information as I came out of town a short time ago,' Moran said. 'It was Bowtell who killed the lieutenant on your orders, Major. I was told the accusation can be proved, so you don't have a leg to stand on, and you must be plain loco if you can't see you're all washed up.'

'If that's the case then all I have to do is kill the witnesses against me. That's you, Moran, the girl, and Sergeant-Major Craven. When that's done I'll be in the clear.'

'You can't murder half the men in this command,' Craven said. 'It looks as if you've left it too late to get out, Major. Put down your gun, sir, and I'll do what's necessary.'

'I'm waiting for a patrol to report in,' Harmon said. 'They are hand-picked men who will take care of you three.'

'So you're to blame for my brother's death!' Ruth's voice rose to a higher note as she spoke.

Before Harmon could reply, Moran heard footsteps outside the office, and a voice called for the Major.

'In here, Chaddock,' Harmon replied, and the door was opened and a sergeant appeared, tall, tough and determined.

'No problems in town, Major,' he reported. 'I saw the men you mentioned and they gave me the all clear. Apart from that, everything is normal.'

'That's good news,' Harmon said. 'There's one other matter for you to handle, and after that you can call it a day. I want you to get rid of some evidence, and then we'll be in the clear. Take the Captain, the Sergeant-Major, and Miss Sandwell out of here and dispose of them.'

Sergeant Chaddock looked at the Sergeant-Major, and a frown crossed his face.

'Do you mean kill them, Major?'

'What else? They've learned too much about what's been going on.' Harmon paused and glared at Chaddock. 'You're not going soft on me, are you, Sergeant?'

'No, sir. Your order will be carried out.'

'Then I'll leave it to you.' Harmon got to his feet. 'I'm going into town now – some unfinished business. I'll be back first thing in the morning. Draw your gun, Chaddock. Captain Moran is highly dangerous at all times, and if you give him half a chance

157

he'll turn the situation on you and you'll be dead.'

Chaddock pulled his gun. Moran tensed. Harmon got up from the desk and moved towards the door, holstering his pistol as he did so. He passed between Moran and Chaddock, and for a brief moment Moran was shielded from the menace of Chaddock's gun. Moran reached out, grasped Harmon's shoulder, and slammed his right fist against Harmon's chin; thrust Harmon against Chaddock and both men went down in a tangle of bodies. Chaddock tried desperately to get his gun clear of Harmon's body to fire a shot at Moran, but Moran stepped in and kicked the pistol out of Chaddock's hand.

Harmon was dazed by Moran's blow. Chaddock disentangled himself from Harmon and lurched to his feet. He halted abruptly when he found himself looking into the muzzle of a gun which Sergeant-Major Craven had pulled out of a desk drawer. Harmon tried to get to his feet but dropped back to the floor. His hand fell by chance upon the pistol that Moran had dropped to the floor and he surged to his feet, trying desperately to cover Moran, who lunged at him.

The crash of a shot hammered through the office. Moran pulled up as if he had run into a brick wall; looked around quickly, and saw Craven motionless, the gun in his hand covering Chaddock. Moran's gaze shifted to Ruth, who was sitting stiffly in her seat by the desk, and a faint twist of gun smoke was rising from the small pocket gun she was holding. Her face was ashen, eyes wide, and she was staring at Major

Harmon, who was swaying on his feet, the weight of the gun in his hand pulling itself out of his grasp. Harmon took a half pace forward, his mouth agape, a thin trickle of blood issuing from between his lips. Then the life ran out of him and he crashed to the floor.

Moran collected his gun from the floor and slid it into his holster.

'Put Chaddock in the guardhouse, Sergeant-Major,' Moran said, and Craven grinned tensely and marched Chaddock out of the office.

Moran bent to examine Harmon, who was dead; a small bullet hole in his neck testified to Ruth's accuracy with a gun. Moran went to the girl and sat down at the desk. He eyed her critically. She was trembling, eyes filled with the turmoil she had experienced.

'You saved my life,' he said gently, 'and not only mine but your own and Craven's. You saved three of us. Who taught you to shoot like that?'

She sat up a little straighter in her seat and her expression changed slightly, as Moran had intended.

'I saved your life,' she said faintly, and shock began to recede from her eyes.

'And I'll always be grateful,' he said gently.

'What happens now? Shall I be charged with shooting him?'

'You shot him in self-defence. He had threatened to murder you, and he was in the act of shooting me when you stopped him. I was about to deal with him when you stepped in. But that's over now, and you can forget about it.'

159

She smiled, and relief began to filter into her face. 'You said he told Bowtell to kill my brother.'

'That's how it was, and Bowtell is dead.' Moran took her arm and gently pulled her to her feet. 'Shall I take you back to town? You'll be safe there now the men running the crooked business are dead or in jail.'

'You've still got work to do to finish your investigation.'

'That can wait a little longer. I can spare time to spend with the woman who saved my life.'

He led her outside, and a sigh escaped him as he looked around. Soon his job here would be finished, so he could take a little time off for himself. And he knew how he could spend it. He would explore his feelings for Ruth, and perhaps he could help her through the bad days she would experience before she could settle down again. He put an arm around her shoulder, and she looked up at him and pushed in closer to his side, as if seeking protection. He liked the contact, and for a moment his thoughts shifted to the future. He relished the thought of getting to know this girl, for their trails had come together and had merged, and relief filled him as they walked closely together through the silent shadows.